About the Author

I am a retired firefighter and police command centre supervisor. I have two grown up sons and two grandsons. I am a widower and my late wife always encouraged me to write. I started writing children's stories for my grandsons and have had one of these published, *The Legend of Tor Silverwolf.* Backlash is my first adult novel and I have drawn heavily on my previous police service experience to make the story as realistic as possible. I am a keen sports fan, especially rugby and cricket and I work as a volunteer for the Yorkshire Wildlife Trust.

Backlash

To Alex.

Many Thanks

Ray.

Ray Fox

Backlash

Olympia Publishers
London

www.olympiapublishers.com
OLYMPIA PAPERBACK EDITION

A CIP catalogue record for this title is
available from the British Library.

ISBN: 978-1-80074-327-4

This is a work of fiction.
Names, characters, places and incidents originate from the writer's
imagination. Any resemblance to actual persons, living or dead, is
purely coincidental.

First Published in 2022

Olympia Publishers
Tallis House
2 Tallis Street
London
EC4Y 0AB

Printed in Great Britain

Dedication

I dedicate this book to my late wife Kathleen. Without her love and support, even now, I would not have had the confidence to write these stories.

Acknowledgements

Thank you to Roger and Alex for their help and encouragement in getting *Backlash* good enough to be accepted for publishing.

Chapter 1

Weybrooke Children's Care Home, January 1985

It was always dark when she came. The stairs creaked as she crept up onto the landing. Heavy laboured breathing could be heard as the footsteps grew ever nearer.

Maybe they won't want me tonight? Maybe she'll choose someone else, the child thought.

The door of the dormitory opened slowly and silently. A thin sliver of light crept menacingly across the threadbare carpet as it penetrated the room. It slowly crawled across the floor like a shimmering monster searching for someone to devour. It stopped next to the bed. The child held its breath and squeezed their eyes even more tightly closed. A figure appeared alongside, blocking out the light and casting a dark shadow onto the bedspread. A thin cold hand reached out and touched the child's shoulder.

"Come with me my sweet," said a husky female voice. "Our daddy is waiting." The hand gripped the shoulder firmly and forced the terrified child out of bed and towards the staircase.

The child was led, shivering, down three flights of stairs and into the cellar. It was called the cellar but, to the child, it was more like a dungeon. A single light bulb hung from a ragged flex in the middle of the ceiling. The light hardly penetrated the darkness. The dim light shone weakly into a small dank room with stark bare flooring and plain brick walls. The atmosphere felt cold and damp, and smelt of old rotting mushrooms. The child trembled in terror, their breath coming in rapid pants. A solitary wooden chair stood across the room in front of the far wall. The child was taken over to it and forced roughly to sit down. The child slumped forward afraid to look up.

"Don't sit there with your head down, look at our daddy," screeched the female.

The child lifted its head slowly and gazed, terrified, across the room. Hanging from the wall opposite was a man. He was naked, except for a leather hood covering his head and shoulders. His wrists were fastened securely by handcuffs to a rusty metal ring that was secured to the crumbling brickwork. His arms were stretched taught above his head, causing his fat body to sag down, motionless. His naked stomach almost covered his exposed genitals it was so large and flabby. He perched on skinny legs which trembled under the strain. He breathed in short excited gasps.

The woman approached the male and spoke in a domineering voice. She was tall and slim, and wore a tight black rubber suit that clung to her body like a second skin. Her legs were covered by long, high-heeled, thigh-length boots. Shoulder-length black gloves completed her costume. Her jet-black hair was pulled back tightly on her head, and even in the dull light it shone like lacquered mahogany. It terminated in a long pigtail that hung loosely down her back, bound tightly at the end by a thin silver chain. She wore heavy, almost white, makeup, with black eye shadow adding dramatically to the already dark of her mad eyes. Her lips were coloured bright red giving her a chilling and macabre appearance, like a grotesque character from a sixties 'Hammer House of Horror' film. In one hand she carried a riding crop that she waved menacingly in front of the male.

Turning to the child she asked.

"Do you know what happens to naughty boys?" The child knew exactly what the answer was, having been forced to witness the bizarre ritual many times before.

"Well, speak up," screamed the woman madly.

"No," replied the child in a feeble voice.

"They have to be punished. don't they?"

"Yes, Mother," whimpered the child.

The woman turned toward the male and shouted. "Have you been a naughty boy, Daddy?"

"Yes, but don't punish me please, Mother," cried the man.

"Oh, but you must be punished," the woman shrieked. "Come here child."

The child sat quite still, as if frozen to the chair by fear.

"I said come here, now!"

Still the child remained motionless. The woman crossed the room and, grabbing the child roughly by the hair, dragged the infant from the chair and over to the man. She thrust the riding crop into the child's trembling hand and whispered menacingly, "Punish him!"

The man tensed, pulling violently at his chains.

"Do it!" screamed the woman and slapped the child viciously across the face. The child raised the crop and slashed down onto the man's body. The male jerked. A long red weal appeared below his left nipple, stretching down across his ample waist. He groaned.

"Again, again!" shouted the woman, "he has not been punished enough yet."

The child, eyes now tightly closed, brought the crop down again, this time catching the man below the waist, slashing his thighs and exposed manhood. The man screamed a curse.

"You are a cruel, fucking bitch."

"Shut up you pathetic little worm," the woman shouted back. "Punish him again for his cursing, child."

The child struck at the man. Again and again the crop landed on the man, the lashes leaving more and more ugly red streaks across the man's pale soft body. The child began to tire.

"Red light, red light," moaned the man.

The woman quickly jumped between the child and the man, snatching the crop from the child's hand. She stared at the man. His body was beaten red raw, the great weals lying like a broken spider's web over his torso. The woman's eyes strayed down to his genitals. An evil glint came into her eyes.

"Do it," she said, forcing the child down towards the man's erect penis.

"Please no," whimpered the child. "Don't make me."

It was warm and safe here. The child lay trembling under the covers thinking all the time, *I will not cry, I will not cry.* Pain ran down the child's arm from the shoulder to the fingers, the muscles burning from the effort of using the whip on the man. The child blocked out the pain and the final sickening action of the event and tried to sleep.

A soft hand crept under the covers and gently stroked the child's back. "Are you all right?" a young voice asked.

"Was it as bad as always?" asked another.

"One day, when I'm grown up and have left this place, I am going to kill them," added a third angry voice.

I have already decided to do that, thought the child. *One day!*

Chapter 2

Dorkshire Police Command Centre, 3rd April 2007

It was Sunday morning, always a quiet time in the Force Command Centre. Susan Sutton sat reading the latest operational order titled, 'Response to Firearms Incidents.' As part of her duties as a call taker in the command centre she was required to keep abreast of all new procedures. She yawned, stretching stiffly, almost disturbing the Oralite headset attached to her left ear. "God this is a bit dry," she muttered to herself. Suddenly the 999 emergency line alarm, automatically beeped in her ear.

"Hello. This is the police emergency service. Can I help you?"

"Oh yes please, I, er, I think I've found a body."

"You think you've found a body madam? OK, let me take a few details and then we'll see what we can do. Are you OK?"

"Yes, I think so, a bit shook up but OK. My dog was scratching around in some undergrowth and came up with a bone. I had a quick look and there are quite a few more there."

"OK we'll come to that in a minute. I have a few questions I need to ask first before we get down to the details. Now, what telephone number are you calling from?"

"I'm on my mobile. The number is 07814878622"

"Just to confirm it is 07814878622?"

"Yes, that's correct."

"And what is your name and address please?"

"Mrs Jayne Wilson. Nineteen The Broadway. Bigton."

"Thank you, Mrs Wilson, now please tell me exactly what has happened."

"Well, I had been walking Teddy, that's my Highland Terrier, he's such a darling you know, a bit mischievous at times but generally a good boy. Anyway, we were in Brumby Woods, just on our way home as a matter of fact, when Teddy suddenly disappeared into some bushes. He started to bark and scratch about. I called to him. 'Teddy, come here at once.' He ignored me, which was unusual as he is normally such an obedient little chap. Anyway, as I pushed into the bushes he reappeared with a bone in his mouth. I was quite shocked really, I mean, it's not what you expect to happen on a quiet Sunday morning is it? He often finds the odd dirty old ball or stick but he's never found a bone before."

"Quite madam," replied the operator. "Now where exactly are you now? I would like to send an officer down to you so you can point out exactly where you found the bones."

"I'm waiting at the entrance to the wood, the one on Alexander Close," replied Mrs Wilson.

"Thank you, Mrs Wilson, please keep your mobile switched on and wait there for the officer. Someone should be with you within fifteen minutes." The operator terminated the call and turned around in response to a question from the duty inspector.

"What have we got Susan?" asked Inspector David Elms. David Elms was the force duty officer for the day. He had been a police officer for twenty-three years, serving first as a beat bobby, then as a traffic officer and finally as a detective sergeant in CID. He was promoted to the rank of inspector two years later and transferred into the Force Command Centre. His role, along with the other four inspectors in charge of the four shifts that made up the staffing of the centre, consisted of overseeing the emergency call-taking procedures and supervising the initial incident response resulting from those calls.

"A woman's reporting she's found some bones, boss," replied Susan.

"Do you think there's anything in it?" the inspector enquired.

"There could be, I suppose."

"OK then. Let's get a patrol to attend. Inform the divisional sergeant and put scenes of crime (SOCO) on standby. I'll ring the duty detective inspector (DI) just in case. You know what CID are like if we don't give them a heads-up early." Inspector Elms dialled the extension number for the DI. It was answered after a couple of rings.

"CID. Detective Sergeant (DS) Hodge speaking."

"Hello Bill, its Dave Elms in the command centre. Who's the duty DI today?"

"Hello boss. The duty DI is Pete Bridle, but he's in a meeting at the moment. Can I help you?"

"Yes. I just wanted to give you an early nod about an incident that's just come in. A woman walking her dog has found some bones over in Brumby Woods. Don't know yet if there's anything in it but we've got a unit en route and uniform supervision is aware."

"Thanks boss, I'll tell the DI. Is there an incident number

we can keep our eye on?"

"Yes, its incident 379 of today," replied Inspector Elms. Dave Elms knew that a member of CID would monitor the incident via the force's computerised command and control system. All information regarding any incident was recorded in this manner. It was updated dynamically, by the officers at the scene, via the command centre radio controllers.

Chapter 3

"Delta Foxtrot one seven a message over," transmitted the radio despatcher from the command centre.

"Delta Foxtrot one seven receiving," replied the police officer whose call sign it was. The officer was constable 1946 Jane Farthing, a uniformed officer with five years police service. She was small and quiet, petite with blonde hair and a fresh complexion. Despite her small stature she was a courageous police officer having already received a commendation for disarming a man with a knife at a domestic dispute on one of the town's more notorious estates. Her colleagues affectionately referred to her as 'Rottie' as she reminded them of a Rottweiler dog, fearless and stubborn, and always reliable in a tight spot.

"Delta Foxtrot one seven can you attend at the Alexander Close entrance to Brumby Woods, there see a lady called Jayne Wilson who has reported her dog finding some bones, over."

"Roger control. ETA about ten minutes," replied PC Farthing.

Thank goodness, she thought, *a job at last.*

"Control from Hotel X-Ray Zero six." (Hotel X-Ray Zero six was the on duty dog handler.)

"Hotel X-ray zero six go ahead," the controller replied.

"Yes, I'm free and close by so I'll attend Brumby Woods as well. My dog may be useful."

"Roger zero six, I'll show you attending," replied the controller, as she entered the dog handler's call sign onto the incident log.

Chapter 4

PC Farthing pulled into the entrance to the wood, booked in attendance with the radio operator, pulled on her uniform hat and, after locking the patrol car, walked over to greet the lady with the small dog. "Hello Mrs Wilson. I understand you've found some bones."

"Well actually it was Teddy who found them, he's my Highland Terrier you know. We were coming home from our walk when he started scratching around. It was then I realised he had dug something up. I'll show you where it was. It's this way." PC Farthing smiled to herself as she followed the elderly woman along the tree lined path.

I hope it's nothing serious, Jane Farthing thought to herself as they entered the cool shade of Brumby Woods. She quickened her steps in order to keep up with Mrs Wilson as she walked briskly along until she came to an area of thick shrubbery.

"It was in there, see," she said, pointing into the centre of the bushes.

Jane was just about to force her way into the bushes when a voice called to her.

"Hang on Jane, you may as well let Lucky and I do that.

We're more suited to tramping around in the bushes." It was Neil Usher, the dog handler, and his German Shepherd dog, Lucky.

"Thanks, Neil. Never did like poking around in dingy places," said Jane, stepping to one side and allowing the handler and dog to push through into the scrub. Mrs Wilson took one look at Lucky and immediately picked up Teddy and clutched him tightly to her chest.

"Don't worry love, he only bites bad guys," said Neil Usher as he disappeared into the bushes. Jane and Mrs Wilson waited for what seemed an eternity for the dog and handler to come out of the bushes. After a while they appeared.

"Well, I don't think it's anything sinister," said Neil as he brushed leaves and dust from his tunic. "It looks like the remains of a dog. As well as the bones, we found some pieces of fur which I suspect are from a large dog. We won't know for sure until SOCO have a look, but I'm pretty sure that's what it is. I tell you what Jane, I'll radio in for SOCO to attend if you like. I can hang around here while you get Mrs Wilson home and take her statement. Lucky could do with some exercise."

"Great. Thanks Neil. I'll see you back at the nick for a cup of tea when you've finished. Now, Mrs Wilson, let's get you home," said Jane. "I think you've had enough excitement for one day."

"And Teddy too," the old lady replied. Jane saw the mischief in Neil's eyes but ignored it.

Neil clicked on the transmit button on his radio and called the despatcher.

Chapter 5

The scenes of crime officer finished his initial examination of the bones and completed photographing the scene. Turning to PC Usher he said, "Well I'm inclined to agree with your opinion Neil. I'm 99.9 % sure it's the remains of a dog, a pretty big one too." Scenes of Crime officers were all trained in basic human anatomy so they were usually confident of the origins of any bones they were asked to identify. "Of course, we won't know for certain until the lab analysis but I don't see why we cannot get the council to collect them and drop them off at the lab. Are you going to hang around until they arrive? I've got a burglary I need to attend to."

"Yes OK. I'll get control to call the council out for the remains, I don't know how long they'll be though, I suppose it will be a call out job being Sunday and all. I'll take Lucky for a walk while they arrive. Come on Lucky, walkies!"

By the time Neil Usher and Lucky had returned to the scene, the council cleansing men were waiting. "Blimey you were quick," he said.

"Yes," replied the older of the two council workers. "We'd just got back to the depot after cleaning up after a road accident, so we didn't have far to come. What have you got for us?"

"It's this way," replied Neil, "an old lady found some bones in the shrubbery." Neil escorted them to the place where the bones lay and watched as they bagged them up.

"Right," said the council worker," that's us done, we're off now."

"So are we," replied Neil, "come Lucky."

There was no sign of the dog. "Lucky. Lucky, here boy," called Neil. He heard a slight yelp coming from the bushes where the bones had been found "What are you doing in there?" he asked.

Neil forced his way back into the bushes where he found Lucky excitedly pawing at the hollow in the ground that the council workers had left.

"What is it boy?" he asked, pulling the dog away. He looked down at the spot where Lucky had been scraping. He gently pushed back some more loose earth and felt a shudder run through his body as his fingers touched something smooth and cold. He gently cleared more debris away until he could make out what his fingers had felt. It was a human arm!

Chapter 6

Southside Police Station, CID Office, April 3rd 2007

"Hello CID office. DS Hodge speaking."

"Hello Sarge, it's the command centre here. Have you seen the latest update on Incident 279?"

"Not for an hour or so, I've been out of the office. The last entry I read said that SOCO thought it was the body of a dog."

"That's correct but there's been a further development. The police dog found what looks like human remains under the dead dog."

"What, under the dog?"

"Yes, it appears so. SOCO are back on scene and we've called out a police surgeon."

"Right thanks. Tell the force duty officer to declare this a major incident. Get as many uniform patrols down there as you can to preserve the scene, I'll break the good news to the DI. That's his Sunday lunch up the spout. We should be there in about half an hour."

"OK Sarge, will do."

Bill Hodge put the phone down, rubbed his stubbly chin and muttered to himself, "A body buried under a dog. Was it deliberate or a bizarre coincidence? I wonder."

He picked the phone up again and dialled the number for Detective Inspector Pete Bridle. When the telephone was answered at the other end he said. "Hi boss its Bill. Do you want the bad news or the bad news?"

"Oh shit. Go ahead Bill," was the anxious reply.

Chapter 7

Brumby Woods 3rd April 2007

Detective Inspector Pete Bridle peered into the hole the scenes of crime officers had excavated around the body. Pete was a tall man, six feet two inches, forty-two years of age, his once slim build now spreading slowly outwards since a knee injury had curtailed most of his sporting activities. He had been in the police for nearly twenty years, the last five heading up the Serious Crime Unit (SCU) He stared intently at the back of the man who was bent over examining the corpse. He knew better than to interrupt a police surgeon during the initial examination of a body and Dr Amir Patel was no exception. Pete Bridle had known Amir for several years and they had worked on a number of suspicious deaths together. After a few minutes the doctor stood up, stretched, and looked at DI Bridle.

"Good morning, Peter. How are you?" he asked.

"Better than that poor sod in there." he replied.

Amir chuckled and stretched out his hand for Pete to help him out. Amir appeared even smaller than his five feet seven inches when standing next to Pete Bridle's six foot two, stocky frame. Despite his slight build, Pete knew Amir was not a man to be trifled with. He had a keen mind and a dogged determination to ferret out the truth, no matter how long it took. Amir pulled off his surgical gloves and discarded them in a waste bag. He pushed his thick, gold-rimmed glasses further up his slightly hooked nose and waited for the inevitable barrage of questions Pete would throw at him.

Pete's steely blue eyes moved quickly from the body to engage the deep, brown ones staring out at him from behind Amir's spectacles.

"How long?"

"Well let's start with what I can say with any degree of certainty. He is a white male, approximately forty-five to fifty years of age. He has dark greying hair and all his teeth. There are no obvious signs of trauma to the body apart from a number of long red marks around the torso and genital area. He also has red marks on both wrists, as if he may have been bound. I do not think, however, that any of these are of sufficient severity to be the cause of death. There would appear to be no items of clothing buried with the body and he isn't wearing any jewellery. He has no tattoos or scars. Now you want the answer to the 64,000-dollar question! How long has he been dead? Well, it's difficult to say really, but judging by the amount the body has decomposed, I would say about four to six weeks."

"Cause of death?" asked Pete.

"No idea," replied Amir. "Like I said before, looking at the body, there are no obvious signs of injury. It could be natural causes."

"Yes, and I could be the next Chief Constable," Pete said. "Maybe it was some type of weird sex game that went wrong? But where does the dog come into it? I assume it was buried on top to put anyone snooping around off the scent. That's a new one on me but we'll check it out," the latter said almost to himself as his brain began to slip into serious crime mode.

"How long before we can get him to the mortuary and get an autopsy done?"

"Well, I've done all I can do here. I suppose it's up to your boys to finish taking photographs and search the area," said Amir. "I'd like to think they could do post mortem tomorrow, but who knows?"

"Thanks, Doc," replied Pete.

"Are you playing golf on Wednesday?" Amir asked. "You know it's the charity game between the police and the hospital staff."

"I was, but judging by this little lot, I think I'll just give a donation and call it a day," Pete replied.

"Well good luck with this. Let me know if there's anything I can do after the autopsy has been done. Bye, Peter."

"Bye, Amir," said Pete turning around to look at the corpse again. "Now mister, who the hell are you and what are you doing here naked with a dog for company?"

Chapter 8

Horkshire General Infirmary, NHS Toxicology Laboratory,
2007

"Hey, Mike, are you coming for a pint after work?" asked Darren Leger, the laboratory team leader.

"No thanks, Darren, I can't, I've got this test to finish then I'm off to the gym," replied Michael Drake.

Mike, as he was known, had worked as a technician at the toxicology lab since he graduated from Melchester University five years previously. He enjoyed the work. His workmates thought he was a bit odd, but good at his job. He was a private person who kept himself to himself and socialised very little. His personnel records showed he had no family and no listed next of kin. He drove a modest car, lived alone in a modest flat and, as far as anyone knew, had no girlfriend.

"No wonder you're all skin and bone," replied Darren. "You spend half your life at that fucking gym. Bet there's a fit young bird there flashing her tits at you."

"I wish," replied Mike, cringing at Darren's crudity.

"Well, have fun," shouted Darren. "Don't forget to lock up, bye."

Mike stretched his thin frame, ran his fingers through his

thick, short-cropped, black hair, sighed, and returned to his work. He knew that all the exercise he took and his strict diet kept him slim but strong. It suited him to be like that. He finished the test procedure he had been carrying out. It was a routine blood test for signs of Malaria. The request had come from a local GP who had a young male patient displaying some unusual symptoms. The doctors had hit the panic button when he realised the male had just returned from a safari holiday in Kenya.

He waited for thirty minutes for the test results to come back, they were negative for Malaria, but showed signs of the male being HIV positive. *He's obviously been with the wrong type of 'wild animals' whilst he was in Africa*, thought Mike. He printed off the results and placed them in Darren's 'Out Tray' before closing down the laboratory and heading for home. He climbed into his dark green Ford Escort car, his nerves jangling with a mix of fear and anticipation. The engine fired first time and Mike Drake drove carefully out of the staff car park and onto the bypass that led home.

Chapter 9

The computer hummed quietly until it responded to the password then soon burst into life, flashing up the 'You have mail.' message onto the screen. The hands moved expertly over the keyboard, selecting the programme which opened the electronic message system. Amongst the list of messages received was one for '**Melinda**.' With a single click the message opened. The user of the computer quickly scanned the message, it read…

Hello Melinda.

I have read your message on the internet, and can reassure you that I have been a really 'BAD BOY!' I would like us to meet so you could teach me how to behave properly. I can come anytime!

I look forward to meeting you.

G.

Melinda opened a new programme attached to the email system. By opening a series of very expensive and illegal sub programmes she was able to trace back the E Mail from G and obtain details of his service provider. Once these details were confirmed the system hacked into the service provider's records and obtained G's personal information. The system then cross-referenced the name against the data bases of all local organisations that dealt with childcare.

After a few moments the system bleeped, indicated a match had been found. "So G, you are a naughty boy," said Melinda in a menacing voice. She closed the programme and returned to the email.

Melinda clicked on the reply button.

Dear G,

Friday. 11.30pm. The address is 47 Armstrong Terrace.

The door will be open. Lock it behind you and follow the stairs down to the cellar. There you will find a table with an envelope on it. Open the envelope, it contains your instructions. Do not tell anyone where you are going! Discretion is vital.

Remember the codeword 'AMBER'.

It was early Monday morning. Three days to get things organised, thought Melinda. She quickly closed the email programme on the computer and brought up Google search. She entered 'Car Dismantlers in Horkshire' and clicked the search button. From the long list which was presented, Melinda scrolled down until she found one that she thought would be suitable. She left the room and went upstairs to change. When she returned, she was wearing a dark hooded fleece, blue jeans and strong walking shoes. On her head she wore a black woollen bobble hat pulled down over her ears and her hands were encased in black surgical gloves. She grabbed her car keys and, making sure the house was secure, headed off on foot to the lock-up she rented.

The car was kept in a garage about a two mile walk from the house. It was an old inconspicuous looking dirty black Volvo 240 estate. The garage formed part of a group of disused industrial units well away from houses and people. Melinda quickly covered the distance on foot, making sure no one saw her leave or followed her. She felt confident that at two in the morning the streets would be deserted. She arrived at the garage and unlocked the door, climbed into the car and drove it out of the garage. Leaving the engine running, she returned to the garage. On the back wall stood a steel locker next to a large chest freezer. She undid the padlock on the locker and, reaching up to the top shelf, took out a plastic bowl, a strong black rubbish sack, and a gallon container of undiluted anti-freeze. Bending down to the bottom of the cabinet she removed some thick leather gloves and a pair of heavy-duty bolt croppers. She locked everything up, returned to the car, and set off for the car dismantlers she had selected.

Chapter 10

The scrap yard was situated off the main road, along a narrow lane. *Out of sight of anyone who might be offended by piles of rusting vehicles,* thought Melinda. She drove past the main gate, turned the car around at the end of the lane, and parked up in the shadows. She waited for twenty minutes to make sure no one had seen her arrive. The yard had limited flood lighting, just enough to illuminate the door to the site office, and the front gate. Carefully Melinda took the items she had brought with her out of the car and approached the chained double main gates. A slight drizzle was falling, giving the impression of smoke drifting across the yard. She shivered nervously despite knowing what to expect. She quickly placed the plastic bowl on the floor and poured a generous amount of concentrated anti- freeze into it. As she finished, she heard a deep menacing growl.

She looked up just as a vicious looking dog rushed at the gate, barking, and snarling threateningly. Melinda quickly pushed the bowl under the gate and stepped back, hoping no one had heard the dog. The dog immediately became quiet and cautiously sniffed the bowl. Melinda watched, fascinated, as the dog, unable to resist the smell of the anti-freeze, began to lap up the contents of the bowl. It was a large, heavyset animal, with scruffy, thick, matted fur. It looked like a cross between a German shepherd and a Doberman, big enough for what she needed. She hoped there was sufficient liquid in the bowl to disable the animal. She looked on anxiously as the dog continued to lap up the fluid, drinking greedily even as it was dying. She waited a few moments, watching carefully as the dog slowly stopped drinking, closed its eyes and lowered its head into the near empty bowl. Once she was certain the dog was dead, she cautiously approached the gates. Quickly donning the heavy leather gauntlets and taking a firm grip on the bolt croppers, she proceeded to cut the chain that secured them. The gates screeched noisily as she pushed them open and, checking for a moment that nothing or anyone had heard the noise, she entered the yard.

Stepping over the lifeless dog she made her way to the office door and, now using the bolt croppers as a lever, attempted to prise it open. She continued, unsuccessfully, to force the door. Gaining entrance was not, however, the object of the exercise. She wanted to cause sufficient damage to the door to give the impression that an attempt had been made to burgle the premises. The irate owner would no doubt report this to the police when he arrived in the morning. The dog's disappearance would be put down to the fact that the gate had been left open after the thieves left. Breathing heavily from her exertions Melinda returned to the dog.

She kicked the motionless body of the dog to ensure it was dead. Opening the black rubbish bag and placing it in front of the prostrate animal, she slowly pulled the bag over the carcass. Still breathing heavily, she dragged the bag to the rear of the car and heaved it into the boot. The rest of the equipment was replaced in the boot and, after a final check round, Melinda drove away, steadily.

Melinda arrived back at the garage where everything appeared just as she had left it. The drizzle seemed a little heavier now, helping to reduce the visibility. *This is good,* she thought, *the mist will help hide my activities.* It had taken her just over an hour to complete the task.

Entering the garage, Melinda went to the rear wall and unlocked the steel locker. Then she opened the lid of the freezer, and straining with effort, managed to carry the dead dog from the car boot into the freezer. She carefully closed the freezer lid. After pausing to catch her breath, she returned to the car, collected the remaining items from the boot, and placed them back into the cabinet, before attaching and locking the padlock She then drove the car back inside, secured the doors, and set off home. "Phase one completed," she said to herself.

It was only after she was back in the car and cold air from the not yet warm heater blew into her face that she realised the woollen hat she had been wearing, was gone. *Now where the hell could that be,* she thought. *Should I go back and try to find it? No, too dangerous. I daren't risk being seen back at the yard.* Melinda knew the hat could be a possible clue, but it was a risk she must take. After all it was only a minor crime at a shady scrap yard and would probably not be investigated too closely. She left the unit block and headed back home.

Chapter 11

Southside Police Station Major Incident Room April 4th

"OK everyone, can we have a bit of quiet please," said DI Pete Bridle to the group of people assembled in front of him. These were the officers of the major incident team that specialised in serious crimes, in this case a suspicious death, and Pete was the leader. "Well, you all know what we're here for. The body of a male was found yesterday buried in Brumby Wood. Initial details are very sketchy and, until we get the results of the post-mortem, we don't know the cause of death. What we do know however, is that he is a white male, approximately forty-five to fifty years of age. He has dark greying hair and all his teeth. There are no obvious signs of trauma to the body apart from a number of long red marks around the body and genital areas. SOCO has organised DNA samples and, of course, we will be checking dental records to try to establish the identity of the male. He has a small tattoo on his left shoulder, a parrot, if I remember, so that will need following up as well. The usual team members to do that please." Two detective constables at the rear of the room nodded their acceptance of the task. "The office manager is Alan Stanton, so everything through him for collating, please. Our first priority is to identify the male and do some background on him. So far, the press, know very little, only what the media officer has told them. Remember people, let's be professional about this as usual and keep expenses down," he said smiling. "We don't want the Superintendent coming down on us about budget overspend again. All claims for overtime etc. as usual to Alan. We all have plenty to be going on with so let's get started."

Just as Pete Bridle finished talking, the door to the incident room opened and in walked Detective Sergeant Bill Hodge. He held up an A4 size manila folder and waved it at DI Bridle.

"I've got the post-mortem report boss," he said, approaching the front of the room.

"Have you read it?" the DI asked.

"Yes sir," replied DS Hodge.

"OK give us a brief report on the result."

Bill Hodge took a deep breath and began his report. "Well, the cause of death has been identified as asphyxiation but, there are no signs of strangulation. The pathologist believes the man may have been paralysed in some way and that prevented him from breathing. If he was poisoned there is no evidence of it. There were no needle marks anywhere on the body and no signs of any sort of poisonous residue in the mouth or throat." Bill paused for a second before adding, "The report states he was probably still alive when he was buried." A shocked silence came over the room as the group absorbed Bill's last comment. Bill continued. "The body showed no evidence of any recent illnesses, in fact the report states that the male's vital organs were all very healthy. A tissue sample has been sent to the toxicology laboratory at Horkshire General Hospital for full analysis."

"What about the marks on the body?" asked the DI.

"The pathologist seems to think they may be from a whip or riding crop of some sort. He stated that they themselves weren't serious enough to cause any real damage to a healthy male and anyway only a couple broke the surface of the skin."

"Some kind of 'kinky sex' maybe?" asked a team member from the back of the room.

"Maybe," said the DI. "Make a note of it and we'll look into that sort of background when we identify who the male is. In the meantime, let's trawl the records for any similar incidents involving asphyxia. Right, let's get to it, Briefing here at 0800 hours tomorrow. Make sure Alan has all your contact mobile phone details etc. Thanks."

"Any information about the dog?" asked Detective constable Karen James.

"What do you mean Karen?" replied the DI.

"Well, it could just be a possibility that, whoever did this, deliberately buried the body beneath the dog. Why do that? Was it to avoid detection of the body? Is it some sort of a ritual? Is the type of dog important? Where did the dog come from? Someone must have owned it?"

"I don't know Karen, but now you've raised these questions, I'd like you to find out if there is any significance to the way the body was buried."

"Me and my big mouth," replied Karen, smiling.

Pete Bridle had worked with Karen before and knew she would always come at a problem from a different angle. He also knew her intimately. They had been having an affair for two years. 'The worst kept secret in the force', some would say. It was officers like Karen and their 'left field approach' that gave the major incident team its diversity. The team members were multi-skilled, and able to work on their own initiative. Intelligence alone was not enough to tackle complex cases like this and Pete knew deep down they would need all their combined skills and intuition to crack this case.

The team dispersed, leaving Pete Bridle and Bill Hodge alone.

"What are you thinking boss?" asked Bill.

"I'm thinking there could be a lot more to this case than meets the eye," replied Pete.

Chapter 12

Horkshire General Infirmary, NHS Toxicology Laboratory, 2007

"Good morning, everyone," said Darren as he swept into the laboratory. "Are we all fit and ready for another eight hours of riotous fun?"

This was Darren Leger's usual morning greeting to the staff at the toxicology lab. It was met with the same stony silence as always. Darren moved to his position at the head of the laboratory bench and switched on his computer. He logged in and checked to see if any work had come in overnight. His eyes immediately went to an item in the list marked '**Urgent**.' He clicked on the item and quickly read the message.

"Something important has just come in. Can you take it please Michael?"

"Yes sure," replied Michael Drake. "What is it?"

"There's a tissue sample in the secure box. It's from the pathology unit. They require a broad spectrum analyse for any toxins."

"Well, that's a lot of help. Couldn't they have been more specific?" grumbled Michael.

"Doesn't look like it," said Darren. "It's from a body the

police found. Cause of death has been established as asphyxia but there are no physical signs of injury. They want a check for anything that may have caused paralysis to the body."

"Oh, I see," replied Michael. "I suppose they want it yesterday?"

"Yes. ASAP."

Michael went to the secure cabinet and retrieved the tissue sample that had been put there by the security staff during the night. The sample was contained in a small glass tube. Michael carried the tube across to his work station. He removed the sample and placed it carefully onto a slide. He put the slide into the computerised spectrometer. Setting the machine for full analyse, he pressed the start button and left the machine to run through its programme whilst he went for some breakfast.

The canteen was fairly quiet when Michael arrived. He selected a bowl of muesli, one slice of wholemeal toast, a small pot of honey and a cup of black coffee. He paid for the food and made his way to an empty table at the rear of the canteen. He sat down and began to eat.

"Blimey, Michael, no wonder you're so skinny, eating that rabbit food. What you need is proper breakfast, like this."

Michael had no need to look up to see who had spoken. He knew as soon as he heard the voice and saw the large plate of bacon and eggs slammed down in front of him that it was Darren.

Why does he have to be such an arsehole? Michael thought. *Just for once I'd like to eat my breakfast in peace.*

"You know me Darren," replied Michael, through clenched teeth. "I'm a slave to my body. And anyway, you know what they say about rabbits!" Darren forced a smile and set about consuming his food.

Michael returned to the laboratory to see how the tests were progressing. To his surprise the machine had stopped running and the printer was churning out the test results. *That was quick*, Michael thought. *It must be clear.* He tore the report off the printer and began to read, not expecting to see anything out of the ordinary. His heart nearly stopped beating and he found his breath coming in quick gasps as his eyes focussed on one word, curare!

Michael quickly folded the paper and thrust it into his pocket. He placed the tissue sample in the incinerator and turned it on. He returned to his work station just as the other team members came back from their break.

Towards the end of the day Darren Leger enquired with Michael how the tests on the tissue sample were going.

"Oh, it's finished. Came back negative, all clear, no trace of any toxins."

"OK thanks. Complete the report and leave it in my tray for signing off would you. They should be pleased with that service. Not sure if they'll like the results though."

Michael filled out the official toxicology report indicating that nothing unusual had been found with the tissue sample. He stamped it with the departmental identifier and, with trembling hands, placed it in Darren's tray. He looked up at the clock and was relieved to see it was leaving time.

"See you tomorrow," he called, out as he collected his coat and headed for the door.

"Right ho," replied Darren. "Don't do anything I wouldn't do."

Michael ignored the response and hurried from the building.

Chapter 13

Karen James sat alongside Helen Marsh, the Force Analyst, and watched, fascinated, as the girl's hands flew across the keyboard. Karen had asked Helen to search all the force's data bases for reports of missing dogs, and records of incidents involving buried dogs. The search covered all reports from the previous five years within a radius of ten miles from the Southside police station. The two women waited patiently as the computer searched for the information. After about ten minutes the computer 'bleeped' and the results were presented on the screen.

"Right, let's see what we've got then," said Helen.

A list of incidents relating to missing dogs appeared first. There was a total of two hundred and ten.

"Oh boy," sighed Karen. "That's all I need, over two hundred to wade through. Let's see how many reports of found dogs are recorded."

Helen scrolled down the screen until she came to the next list. This showed that there had been seven recorded incidents relating to buried dogs within the last five years.

"That's better," said Karen. "Can we see the full reports on the buried dogs?"

"Yes easily. You just highlight them on the list, click on them and they open. Just like this," said Helen as she proceeded to open the first record.

Karen looked intently at the report. "Excellent," she said. "It shows the exact time and place the dog was found, also an educated guess at the breed of dog. Could you send everything to my terminal at the incident room please?"

"No problem," replied Helen. "It will be there before you get back."

"Thanks for all your help, Helen," said Karen heading for the door.

"Any time," said Helen, "any time at all." Then in a quiet whisper. "Why are the nice ones always straight?"

Karen climbed into her car and took out her mobile. She quickly found the speed dial number she wanted and listened as it rang out at the other end.

"Hello," answered a male voice.

"Are we still on for tonight?" Karen asked.

"Yes, usual time?"

"OK I'll see you then, bye."

Bringing her mind back onto the job, Karen started her car and headed back to the incident room. *I wonder what this will throw up when I check it out,* she thought to herself.

Chapter 14

47 Armstrong Terrace

'G' sat in his car, staring straight ahead through the condensation which had collected on the inside of the windscreen. He was parked well away from any streetlights, just around the corner from Armstrong Terrace. His car was a standard Vauxhall Astra, nothing out of the ordinary, the dark blue colour blending in easily with the shadows. It seemed to him to be a quiet part of town, not many cars or pedestrians passing by. He looked anxiously at his watch again, it showed 11.20 p.m. *Not long now*, he thought, *I wonder what she will be like?* In his nearside wing mirror, he noticed a dark clad figure approaching toward the car. *Could this be her?* G thought. The figure carried on walking past the car and on towards the entrance to the terrace. He heard a voice calling. "Here Bobby, where are you, you silly cat?"

No, he thought, *false alarm, just someone looking for their cat.* The figure carried on along the street and eventually disappeared from view. He checked his watch again, 11.28 p.m. *Near enough*, he thought, and opened the car door.

His hands trembled as he silently closed and locked the car door. He pulled the hood of the camel haired duffle coat he was wearing up over his head, and walked off towards Armstrong Terrace, staring around nervously. His trainers made no sound as he walked to the entrance of the terrace. Reaching it, he took a deep breath, and turned swiftly to his left. The terrace was long and narrow, the only light provided by a single streetlamp about halfway down. He could just make out the numbers on the battered doors of the cramped houses of the terrace. He walked cautiously into the terrace, glancing only briefly to check the numbers of the houses. He paused outside number fifteen, the one next door was number seventeen. *Good*, he thought, *odd numbers on this side* and he set off further down the terrace. After a few minutes he stopped, staring at a dark coloured door with flaking paint. He could just make out the number forty-seven. "This is it," he said to himself, swallowing nervously. He walked up the uneven paved path, placed one gloved hand onto the door handle, turned and pushed. The door opened with a stiff creak.

The door led into a dark passageway. 'G' entered. He stood for a second, removing his hood as he strained to hear any sound. Allowing his eyes to become accustomed to the light and ensuring nothing stirred he moved cautiously down the passageway. He noticed a door at the end of the passage, its shape outlined by the light percolating through the gaps around the edge of the frame. He walked slowly towards it. Pinned to the door was an envelope with the letter 'G' printed on it. He pulled off his gloves and stuffed them into his coat pocket. Hands trembling, he tore open the envelope and removed a piece of folded paper. He held the paper up to the door where the crack allowed light to filter out. He could just make out the printed message. It read…

'GO THROUGH THE DOOR, DOWN THE STAIRS AND INTO THE CELLAR.

THERE YOU WILL FIND A TABLE AND A CHAIR.

ON THE TABLE YOU WILL FIND A MASK AND A PAIR OF HANDCUFFS.

REMOVE ALL YOUR CLOTHES AND LEAVE THEM FOLDED NEATLY ON THE CHAIR!

ON THE WALL ACROSS FROM THE TABLE YOU WILL SEE A METAL RING.

GO TO THE RING, PUT ON THE HANDCUFFS AND MASK.

SHACKLE YOURSELF TO THE RING AND WAIT!'

'G' went through the door and down the stairs. A small powered light bulb suspended from a single wire pendant provided the only illumination in the room. It felt very cold and smelt damp and fusty. He found the items on the table and nervously picked them up to examine them. He replaced them on the table and slowly undressed. The damp atmosphere washed over his warm skin, instantly turning it cold and clammy. A rash of 'Goose Pimples' appeared over his body, the result of the cold and his heightened excitement. He took the mask and handcuffs and walked nervously over to the wall. He gazed up at the metal ring then pulled on the mask. The mask covered the whole of his head, preventing him from seeing anything. After a struggle he managed to attach himself to the ring. His breathing was restricted, making him gasp for breath. He waited in silence, hanging from the wall wondering, what would happen next. This was the first time he had visited a dominant and the web site had described her as strong and beautiful! He was a little scared but aroused too. He knew this is what he had wanted. He had realised in his youth that his needs were different to those of his friends. The few girls he had been with did not understand his anxious fumbling and accused him of being a weirdo when he asked them to perform what they considered to be 'pervy' acts on him. This would put things right. Suddenly he heard a sound, footsteps, coming down the stairs. She was here!

Chapter 15

Melinda had arrived at forty-seven Armstrong Terrace at ten p.m. She liked to be early for her appointments. *Don't like to keep the naughty boys waiting do we*, she thought, *not professional*. She had parked some way off, down a dimly lit side street, and walked to the house. The darkness was her friend. She entered the grubby dwelling from the 'Ten Foot' at the rear, scrambling over the rubbish that had accumulated there through years of neglect and vandalism. She was not too concerned about being seen by the neighbours, they were mostly just groups of drunks and druggies squatting in empty houses adjacent to number forty-seven. She suspected that even if they did see her, they would be in no fit state to remember her or give any sort of description. She had come to the rear entrance as it allowed her to approach the house through a labyrinth of dark alleys leading from the street. In that way it would make it difficult for anyone to establish where a person entering the alley might be going. She unlocked the back door and entered the kitchen. It was cold and smelled of stale food and urine. Locking the door after her, she made her way through the darkness, across the kitchen, into the hallway, and up the stairs. Only when she entered the sparsely furnished bedroom with the thick velvet curtains tightly closed, did she switch on a light.

She looked around the room. A single camp bed, covered by a crumpled sleeping bag, was pushed into one corner. An old wardrobe leaned crookedly against a wall and a shabby dressing table, complete with cracked mirror, stood opposite it. Melinda took off her coat and hung it inside the wardrobe. She removed the clothes that were hanging there and laid them on the bed. She checked her watch. *Plenty of time*, she thought as she began to undress.

She enjoyed the feel of the cool air on her body as she stood naked in front of the mirror. A black rubber suit hung limply from one hand. As much as she enjoyed the sensation of being nude, she knew she must quickly put on the skin-tight suit before the cold air made her body too damp for the material to slide smoothly over it. She squeezed into the suit, the tightness almost taking her breath away. It fitted closely around her neck, sweeping down to cover her shoulders, arms, and hands and flattening her small breasts against her chest. She slid the material down between her legs and carefully fastened the press studs together under her crotch. With difficulty she sat on the bed and pulled on the black, thigh-length, plastic boots. The shiny black of the material contrasted vividly with the white flesh of her smooth thighs. When she stood, the boots stiletto heels made her look even taller than she already was. She pulled out a small stool from beneath the dressing table, sat down and pulled open a drawer. She removed a cosmetics bag and proceeded to apply makeup. Vivid red lipstick contrasted starkly with cream blusher, and dark blue eyeshadow. A thick black wig completed the transformation.

Standing, she gazed approvingly at her image in the mirror. An evil smile flicked crossed her lips as she heard the front door open. She returned to the wardrobe and removed a long riding crop. With a vicious swish she flashed the thin leather stick across the empty space in front of her. She laid the crop down before pulling the bed out of the corner. Once the bed was clear of the wall, she lifted the corner of the threadbare carpet to reveal the floorboards. Pushing gently on one end of a floorboard, she levered the board up. Reaching into the space beneath, she removed another riding crop and a grease proof paper parcel. She took the crop and the parcel over to the dressing table.

With great care she unwrapped the paper to reveal a sticky, dark brown, paste. Taking the second riding crop she rubbed the thin, slashing end, into the paste. She held it up to the light to check there was sufficient paste smeared onto its surface. Satisfied, she put the crop gently onto the dressing table, rewrapped the paste, and returned it under the floor. She replaced the floorboard and pushed the bed back into place. Gathering up both riding crops she took a final look in the mirror, smiled, and left the room.

Now we'll make sure that this naughty boy gets what he deserves, she thought, as she moved slowly down the stairs.

Chapter 16

Karen arrived back at the incident room later than she expected. She hustled into the office, huffing and puffing, and headed straight for the coffee machine. Filling a paper cup with the muddy coloured liquid, she glanced around to see who was still there. A couple of DCs were huddled over their computers and Alan Stanton, the office manager, was sat at his desk, talking on the telephone. He finished his conversation and looked over to Karen.

"How's it going?" he asked her cheerfully.

"Well, if our traffic department ever manage to sort out the congestion on our roads and I could get a bloody parking space in the yard, it would be going better. Do you know, Alan, there are cars in that yard that belong to people who work at HQ? They leave them here and cycle into town. Bloody cheek! They'd be the first to complain if it was the other way round."

"We've always had a parking problem here. Ever since we started to pay decent wages and coppers could all afford cars," Alan said with a smirk. "In my day we only earned a couple of bob a week, so we only needed a large bike shed."

Karen smiled and realised Alan was having fun at her expense.

"OK smart arse. Can I borrow your bicycle clips?" Karen joked, in reply.

"Certainly, they're in my desk drawer gathering dust."

Karen lobbed her empty coffee cup in Alan's direction. He swayed effortlessly to one side, caught the cup, and deposited it in his waste bin in one smooth movement.

"Cheers Alan," said Karen and sat down at her desk and switched on her computer.

The computer quickly booted up and Karen waited patiently as the information she required gradually appeared on the screen. She browsed the incidents involving buried dogs, making a brief list on her note pad as she went through them. She left her desk and walked over to the large wall map that was being used to indicate any places relevant to the enquiry. At present there was only one marker on the map. A yellow pin indicated the place where the man's body had been located, Brumby Wood.

Karen identified the locations where the remains of the dogs had been found and marked them on the map using red pins. When she had finished, she stepped back to see if the seven red pins formed any sort of a pattern. They didn't. *Great*, she thought. The only thing she could safely say was that they were all buried in woods or copse. "Buried them in those locations, to avoid anyone seeing them do it?" she muttered to herself. She sensed someone standing behind her, it was Alan.

"What are those?" he asked.

"They indicate the places where the remains of dogs have been found," she replied.

"Do you think they have any connection to the case," Alan asked.

"Not sure really, but it's something we need to take into

consideration," Karen replied thoughtfully. "I need to check the reports on each missing dog to see if there are any similarities in how and why they all went missing, then see if I can find any connections with the burial sites. That should take me the rest of the week. Hey ho, best get on."

Karen returned to her desk and began to trawl through the two hundred records of missing dogs. She quickly reduced the list by deleting any reports of missing small dogs and any that had subsequently been found. When she had finished the first cull the list had shrunk to just over fifty. On a hunch she checked for any dogs that had been classed as 'guard dogs.' *They were usually large beasts,* she thought. She narrowed this down to twenty. Picking up the telephone she dialled the extension for Helen Marsh. Helen answered after a couple of rings.

"Hi Helen, it's Karen again. Have you got a moment, I'd like to run something by you?"

"Sure, go ahead," replied Helen.

Chapter 17

Karen stopped to check herself in the mirror on the way to answer her apartment doorbell. Her hand brushed a careless strand of hair off her face and she pouted her lips to check the lipstick had not smudged. The red silk, knee length negligee flowed silently around her as she moved down the hallway. Underneath the negligee she wore a pair of sexy, red French knickers with a matching lacy underwired bra. She needed something to help accentuate her small breasts, not that Pete complained, he always said that he could play happily with her tits all night! She opened the door.

Pete stood there leaning against the door frame, smiling, a bottle of Italian Prosecco wine clutched in his hand.

"Hi gorgeous, have you missed me?" he asked, pulling Karen into his arms and kissing her passionately.

"Not out here, the neighbours will see," said Karen, disentangling herself from Pete's arms.

"Fuck the neighbours," said Pete happily, "come here." He made a grab for Karen but she was too quick for him and darted back into the room giggling. Pete followed, shutting the door behind him and throwing off his coat. He reached for Karen who had stopped and turned towards him. "I've missed you," he said.

"I've missed you too, handsome, now, get your clothes off whilst I get some glasses." With that Karen took the bottle from Pete's hand and disappeared into the kitchen.

Pete went into the bedroom and stripped down to his boxer shorts. He glanced at his reflection in the mirror and sighed. "Letting yourself go old son," he said to himself, patting his soft flabby stomach.

"Yes, I can remember when you had a 'six pack', it only seems like a couple of years ago," said Karen mischievously as she came through the door.

"It's you, you've made me soft," replied Pete.

"Well now that will never do, will it?" Karen said with a wink. "Now come here."

Later they lay exhausted, wrapped in each other's arms. There was no need to talk. The closeness they felt made speech unnecessary. It was as if the whole world was at peace and they floated on a soft warm bubble of love. Karen eventually heard Pete's soft deep breathing. Propping herself up on one shoulder she looked down at the man she loved, sleeping gently. Loved but could never have. A lump formed in her throat, and a tear silently trickled, unchecked, down her cheek.

"Stop it, you silly cow," she said silently to herself. "You knew what you were getting into when you started this."

Pete had at first resisted her advances and only began the affair on the understanding that Karen knew that he would never leave his family. His wife Jennifer had MS. Karen knew Jennifer and the two children were totally reliant on Pete for everything. Karen knew Pete loved her, but she also knew he loved his family more. She accepted this but, as time went by and her love for Pete became deeper, it became increasingly difficult for Karen to live with. She had thought about breaking it off, several times, but the idea of not being with him again was unbearable. "You've made your bed young lady," she said to herself, and gently shook Pete awake.

He opened his eyes, smiled at her, and said, "What does a bloke have to do to get a drink in this pub, shag the landlady?"

Karen punched him playfully and reached for the glasses.

They showered together, washing each other gently with sweet smelling bath oil. They made love again, slowly this time, lingering under the hot steaming cascade of water that caressed their newly cleaned bodies. Later they relaxed, naked, on the sofa, in front of the fire, their flesh still tingling from being dried on soft fluffy towels.

"I love you," said Karen, snuggling up under the arm that Pete had draped protectively around her shoulder.

"I know you do," he replied quietly, "and I wish that things were different so we could be together." His voice trailed off sadly.

Karen sat silently for a few moments, enjoying his closeness. She knew what was coming.

"I should go," he said, and eased Karen upright.

She sat on her own, looking into the fire, listening to the sound of Pete dressing in the bedroom. He returned and she turned her face upwards to receive his farewell kiss.

"Bye," he said.

"Bye," she replied and returned her face to the fire.

Pete left, silently closing the door behind him, and headed for the lift. He hated leaving her. The lift was already waiting and he entered it, pressed the button for the ground floor, and turned on his mobile phone. Immediately it bleeped. He checked the message. It was from Bill, asking him to ring in.

Pete looked at his watch, it was 8.45 p.m. *Bill will have left the office by now*, he thought, *only one message so it can't be that urgent. It will wait until the morning.* The lift stopped at the ground floor. Pete waited until the doors slid smoothly open, then left the building, wearily climbed into his car, and went home.

Chapter 18

47 Armstrong Terrace

Melinda pushed open the door to the cellar and went down the stairs. She could see the man shackled to the wall, naked. He was turning his head from side to side, trying to pick up any sounds. He stopped and turned his face towards her.

"Who's there?" he asked, his voice trembling. "Melinda, is that you?"

Melinda walked across the room and stood silently in front of the man.

"Melinda. How dare you call me Melinda?" she screamed into his face. "Only good boys get to call me that and you are not a good boy, are you? Naughty boys have to call me Mother!" With that she reached out and grasped one of the nipples on the man's chest and twisted viciously until he cried out. "Now what do you call me you naughty boy?"

"Mother," he replied quickly.

"Good, that's more like it," Melinda said, "but I still think you have been a very naughty boy and deserve punishing properly. What do you think?"

"Yes Mother," he panted.

Melinda raised the clean riding crop and brought it down

across the man's chest. He gasped in pain and shock. "That's for your bad manners," she said. "Didn't mother teach you to say please?"

"Yes, I'm sorry, Mother."

"Still not good enough," said Melinda slashing the man once more across the chest. Again, the man gasped and his body sagged slightly as he bent in pain.

"Do you think you have been punished enough? You naughty boy," Melinda screamed as she waved the crop in front of his face, close enough for him to feel the draught as it flew past.

"No Mother, I have been really naughty and deserve to be chastised some more."

Melinda stood back and looked at the man. "You pathetic piece of shit," she shouted and commenced flaying the man mercilessly.

The man at first seemed to enjoy the pain, repeatedly moaning "Yes, Yes," as the crop slashed across his body, but his demeanour changed as the pain increased.

"AMBER.AMBER," he cried.

Melinda stopped, breathless. She lowered the crop and glared in disgust at the man hanging limply from the wall. He was sobbing quietly. Melinda reached forward and roughly yanked the man's head back. She ripped off the hood and watched as he blinked at her.

My God she is grotesque, he exclaimed to himself. *What have I done?*

"Let me go," he shouted. "Leave me alone. Help Help!"

"You can shout all you like, naughty boy. No one will hear you," said Melinda. "And anyway, I haven't finished punishing you yet."

"What are you going to do? Keep away from me you cow," he spat.

"Tut, tut, now that's no way to talk to Mother, you naughty boy."

'G' looked on terrified as Melinda threw down the crop and walked over to the table. She carefully picked up the second whip and, with an evil glint in her eyes, returned to the now panic-stricken man. Melinda looked at the man's body. The whip marks were turning deep scarlet, but she was satisfied that none of them had broken the surface of the skin.

She raised the second crop and slashed down hard across the man's thigh. He screamed. She watched fascinated as a trickle of blood oozed from where the crop had bitten into the flesh. The man remained silent. Slowly he began to tremble. His face paled and beads of sweat formed on his brow. The trembling got worse until it turned into a violent spasm. The man shuddered and, searching out Melinda's eyes, begged. "What have you done to me?"

Melinda smiled, "Why, naughty boy, I have only given you what you asked for and deserved," she said. She turned and walked away from the now desperate man.

"Please stop. Don't leave me here," he begged, his voice weaker now.

Melinda switched out the cellar light and made her way back upstairs. She would be back later when the drug had taken effect.

Chapter 19

Pete dropped the children off at school on his way to work, the youngest, George, holding tightly onto his older sister Charlotte's hand. He remained parked outside the school watching the kids play until the bell sounded to summons them inside. His thoughts raced around his head like an out-of-control railway engine, careering downhill. He was torn between guilt and euphoria. He had left Jenny tucked up in bed, the drugs she took for the MS caused her to sleep longer than the rest of them. The nurse would be round later to get her up and dressed. He hated leaving her like that. In fact, he hated himself more every day for the way his life was. He was unsure if Jenny was aware that he was having an affair so he wanted to keep it quiet so as not to hurt her. As the Multiple Sclerosis had progressed and it became clear that they could no longer enjoy a full loving relationship, Jenny had told him that she would understand if he needed to find physical comfort with another woman. He had scoffed at this, telling her with tears in his eyes, that he would never need to and their love was all that mattered. Unfortunately, as time went by, he did feel the need for physical love and despite resisting temptation for a long time he eventually succumbed to the subtle charms of

Karen James. This was where he was now: in love with two women but for different reasons. Jenny was his wife, the mother of his children and his first love. He would always love her no matter what, and he would never leave her and the children. He also loved Karen. She excited him, stimulated him and allowed him to escape the madness of his work and home life. Karen knew that he would never leave Jenny or the kids until...

"Come on," he said to himself, "snap out of it. It hasn't come to that yet." He slammed the car into gear and pulled out into the traffic and headed off to work. *Work,* he thought, *I wonder what delights are waiting for me there?*

Traffic was light and he arrived at the incident room just after nine thirty. The room was full. Everyone turned to look at him expectantly. "Nice to see you're all keen and here before the boss," Pete said, "any chance of a coffee?"

Karen stood up from her desk, went over to the machine and poured a black coffee. "Do you want any milk or sugar boss?"

Pete only just stopped himself from telling Karen that she should know how he liked his coffee as she had made it enough times. He glanced at her and saw the wicked twinkle in her eyes.

"White, no sugar please," Pete replied.

Karen brought the coffee over to his desk where he now sat. She leaned over to put the drink down and whispered in his ear. "The reason we're all here early is because you told us there would be an eight o'clock briefing."

"Oh shit," he muttered. "I'm sorry I'm late folks. I had to drop the kids off at school. Now, let's get on with the briefing. Alan, would you like to start?" Alan Stanton stood, but before he could begin to speak, Bill Hodge stood up.

"I'm sorry to interrupt Alan, but I've got some news."

Alan Stanton sat back down, and Bill began. It was an unwritten rule amongst the team that anyone with anything important to say would just dive in and say it.

"We've identified the body," Bill said. The room remained silent as Bill walked to the front of the office and stood in front of the briefing. He pinned a photograph of the dead man to the board and wrote a name underneath it.

"His name is Clive Wilkinson, fifty-two years old, from thirty-two Welbeck Grove. We got the information from his dental records. He lives with his mother who reported him missing about five weeks ago. I've obtained a copy of the 'Misper File' from Graham Johnson, the missing person officer. He told me the usual checks had been done and Wilkinson has been circulated as a missing person (Misper) on PNC (Police National Computer). He worked as administrative clerk at the local council rates office. He has no criminal record."

"Thanks Bill. Alan, can you allocate two of the team to attend the address and speak with his mother. Make sure they take a family liaison officer with them. Please ensure a thorough search of the premises is carried out. If the guy has a computer bring it back to the Technical Support Unit, (TSU). I'd like their guys to check it over. OK. Anyone got anything else?"

Karen raised her hand. "Yes Karen?" asked Pete.

"I've been following up on the dog angle and I think I may have come across some sort of a pattern," she said.

"Let's hear it then," said Pete.

"Well. I've looked at how many missing dogs we have

had reported within a five-mile radius of our patch over the past few years. As you can imagine there were hundreds. In order to try to narrow it down, I then checked to see how many buried dogs had been found and reported. That number was less. I checked the locations where these were found and discovered they were all buried in remote wooded areas. Because the latest dog to be found was quite large, presumably to cover the body underneath, I now intend to check how many of the dogs that were found were large animals, I'm also trying to establish if there is any pattern as to where the dogs disappeared from. Large dogs are often used to guard premises, maybe security patrol dogs, that type of thing. I know it's a long shot, but I'll give it a bash. I was also thinking maybe we should try and establish how the dog we dug up had died."

"OK that's fine with me," replied Pete. "Alan, can you check everyone is gainfully employed. And I'll catch up with you a bit later. Thanks everyone."

Pete stood up and walked over to the wall board. "Well Mr Wilkinson, what have you been up to then, you naughty boy!" he said to no one in particular.

Chapter 20

The dog was frozen solid, which made dragging it out of the freezer much easier. Melinda was dressed in a dark tracksuit with a hooded top which covered her head, black trainers and she wore thick leather gloves. Hauling the carcass out of the freezer, she hastily wrapped it in an old blanket that she kept especially for this task. It was dark outside. She switched off the internal light to the garage before opening the door and carried the carcass to the rear of her car. Glancing around, she flipped the tail gate up and tossed the bundle onto the rubber matting which covered the boot floor. She returned to the lock up and retrieved a pick and shovel from behind the door. She secured the garage behind her. placed the tools in the boot and set off for forty-seven Armstrong Terrace. As she drove carefully away from the garage area, she thought about the location she had found a few weeks earlier. It was a remote copse lying off a quiet back lane just north of the town. She had studied the location at different times, over a period of days, to establish how often the lane was used. It was usually quiet during the day, only the occasional farm vehicle, trundling along to the adjoining fields, to disturb the peace and tranquillity of the rural setting. It was even quieter during the early evening and she had seen no one at all during the nights she had spent down there. *Another perfect spot*, she thought to herself as she approached Armstrong Terrace.

She parked the car in a different location. "Can't be too careful," she said to herself. She made her way through the back alleys to the rear of the terrace. She unlocked the back door and made her way upstairs to the bedroom before going down to the cellar. Standing in front of the cellar door she took a deep breath before pushing it open and looking inside. The male hung motionless from the ring in the wall. She could see the marks on his wrists where the manacles had bitten into his flesh. His mouth had dropped open and his tongue protruded out at a peculiar angle from one side. She approached silently and gazed into the staring eyes that displayed no signs of life. Her fingers probed on the neck for any sign of a pulse. The flesh was cold and clammy to her touch. She felt no throbbing vein beneath her warm fingers. Glancing down she looked toward the chest, it was totally still, no tell-tale rising or falling. She bent her head toward the man's mouth. No sound of air being dragged down into empty lungs. DEAD!

Reaching into her pocket she pulled out a key ring. She selected a small chrome key and slid it into the hole on the handcuffs. The body slumped to one side as an arm became free, released from its restraint by a quick twist of the key. She unlocked the second wrist and the now, unsupported, body tumbled to the dusty floor. Melinda looked down at the man feeling no remorse. She unzipped the sleeping bag she had brought down from the bedroom and spread it out beside the motionless figure. With apparent ease, she rolled the body onto the bag, folded the bag closed and zipped it up. She gathered up the man's clothing, his wallet and car keys, and placed them into a separate smaller carrier bag. She would sort those out at home. She dragged the sleeping bag and its grisly contents to the top of the stairs. She laid the bundle on the landing floor, hanging half-way over the top stair. She had found by previous experience that this was the easiest way to get the body onto her shoulders. She could then carry it through the house like a fireman rescuing a stricken victim from a burning inferno. *There's only one inferno you're going to*, she thought, *and that's to hell!*

It was still dark. Nothing stirred as she stood at the back door of the house making sure her departure would go unseen. The bundle across her shoulders seemed not to impede her as she carefully picked her way across the rubbish strewn yard and out into the alley. The car was parked close by and she quickly returned to it. Effortlessly she adjusted her load slightly. She opened the car's tail gate with one hand and dropped the body on top of the dog. She closed the tail gate, jumped into the driving seat, and drove off into the night.

Traffic was light. She drove at the legal limit so as not to bring attention to herself. She stopped at a red traffic light. A vehicle pulled up alongside her car. She glanced furtively across and her heart skipped a beat. It was a police patrol car. She remained still, looking straight ahead. The nearside window of the police car opened and a uniform-clad arm indicated to her to open her window. She rolled down her window and looked at the police officer who had signalled to her.

"Mind if I ask what you are doing out at this time of the morning?" he said.

"I'm on my way home. I'm not feeling well so my boss sent me home early," she replied.

"Where do you work then?"

"At the hospital, I'm a night porter."

Suddenly their conversation was interrupted by the police officer driving the patrol car.

"Come on John, we've got a call. There's a burglar alarm sounding over on Smithson Drive. Might be something, that's where all those previous jobs happened."

"OK," replied his passenger. Turning back to Melinda he said, "Make sure you get yourself off home now, no hanging about."

"I will," she said, "and thanks."

The police car turned right at the lights and sped off. Melinda managed to keep her hands from shaking too badly as she engaged first gear and pulled jerkily away.

"What was all that about then John?" asked PC Andy Rawding, as he accelerated the car down the road.

"Just another poor bloody night worker like us, sent home from work early, feeling poorly," replied his partner.

"Lucky bugger. Where does she work?"

"She said she was a porter at the local hospital."

"Oh right. I didn't know they employed women as porters."

"Must do, I suppose it's probably part of the new equal ops. regulations." replied John.

"Have you done the course yet?" Andy asked.

"Yes," replied John," it was a total load of bollocks."

Andy laughed and returned his concentration to driving.

Melinda drove on, constantly checking her rear mirror for any signs of being followed. She breathed a sigh of relief when she eventually left the street lighting behind and headed out into the countryside. It took thirty minutes of careful driving before she arrived at her destination. The lane was dark and empty, as she knew it would be. She pulled the car off the road, parking it behind a thick clump of bushes on firm ground to ensure no tyre tracks were left. She got out of the car and went round to the rear. She opened the tail gate, rummaged around, and pulled out the pick, the shovel, a torch and a pair of wellington boots. Removing her trainers, she tossed them into the back of the car, donned the wellingtons and a pair of heavy-duty work gloves and strode off into the trees.

The spot she was looking for was set back from the lane, about fifty metres into the trees. It was a small clearing with a thick lumpy covering of grass. Melinda placed the shovel and torch on the ground and began to remove the turf with the pick. She cut out a section about two metres by one metre, lying the grass sods carefully faced down ready to be replaced when the digging was finished. It took her about an hour to dig down to the depth she needed to accommodate the two corpses. She was glad of all those hours spent in the gym, pumping iron. Her hands became sweaty inside her gloves as she neared the finish of her task. Climbing out of the hole she stood for a moment to catch her breath and admire her handiwork.

She returned to the car and lifted out the sleeping bag and its contents, placing them on the ground beside the car. Next, she lifted out the blanket containing the dog's corpse and carried it into the trees. She could feel the dog's flesh through the material, softening as it defrosted. At the hole she laid the dog down and returned to the car for the sleeping bag. It took her a little while to carry it back into the small copse and her arms ached with the effort. She dumped the sleeping bag onto the floor, unzipped it to reveal the corpse. Using the torch for illumination she carefully checked the body to make sure there were no tell tales clues left on it. With hardly any effort now she rolled it into the hole. She covered the body with a thick layer of soil. Next, she removed the dog's body from the blanket and tossed it into the grave. She covered it with the remaining soil from the excavation. Finally, she replaced the turf and firmed it down using the shovel. In a couple of days, she knew the grass would begin to grow again, knitting the sods of earth back together. In a short time, the mound would flatten becoming once again part of the clearing. Gathering all the items she had brought with her, and after a final check around, she left the graveside without a thought for the poor souls buried there.

Chapter 21

Bill Hodge, Dave Reeves and a uniformed family liaison officer arrived at thirty-two Welbeck Road, the home of the deceased man, Clive Wilkinson. Bill approached the front door and rang the bell. Through the frosted glass he watched a small, stooped, figure slowly move down the hallway to answer his ring. The door opened on a chain, to reveal a slightly built lady, in her late sixties guessed Bill, wearing a dowdy grey matching skirt and cardigan. Her silver/grey hair was cut short in a bob and her face paled visibly as she looked from Bill to Dave and then the uniformed officer. She removed the chain and opened the door.

Stepping back, she gasped "Oh my God it's Clive, isn't it?" and fell into a dead faint. Bill rushed forward, just managing to catch the woman before she crashed against the staircase behind her. With Dave's help he carried the woman into the front room and placed her gently on the sofa.

"Call for an ambulance will you please?" Bill asked the uniformed officer.

The ambulance arrived within ten minutes, by which time Mrs Wilkinson had regained consciousness. She was checked over by the attending paramedics who advised she be taken to the hospital for a full check-up. She refused, stating she was all right and did not want to make a fuss. She asked Bill about her son. He explained that a body had been found that might be her son, but that it would need to be formally identified by a relative. Bill asked if there was anyone who could do this apart from Mrs Wilkinson. She explained she was a widow, without any other relatives, and that Clive was her only son. She stated she wished to see him. Bill agreed on the condition she go to the hospital first to be checked over. If the doctor said she was strong enough then the uniformed officer would take her to see the body. She agreed to this and left the house in the ambulance, escorted by the uniform PC. She had agreed to allow Bill and Dave look at her son's room.

The room was nothing special. It was just a room with a bed, a wardrobe, a chest of drawers and computer workstation. There were no pictures on the walls, no signs of any childhood memories or souvenirs, nothing. The drawers contained neat piles of clothing, as did the wardrobe. Bill looked at the computer.

"Maybe this can tell us something about Mr Wilkinson," said Bill. "Give us a hand with it will you Dave?" Between them they loaded the computer and its processor into the car and, after securing the house, headed back to the incident room.

"What about the old lady?" Dave asked.

"We'll speak to her later, after she's identified the body," replied Bill. "In the meantime, we'll get this lot back to the technical support guys."

Chapter 22

Karen contacted the scenes of crime office to establish where the remains of the dog that had been buried, along with Clive Wilkinson, had been taken. She was told it had been removed by the council workers who attended the initial report of a found dog. "I hope I'm not too late," said Karen to herself as she replaced the telephone handset and reached for a directory to find the number of the council waste disposal unit. She located a central number and dialled it. A pleasant and helpful council switchboard operator soon located the department Karen needed and transferred her through. A gruff-voiced male answered. Karen explained who she was and what she wanted. The man, who turned out to be the depot foreman, rather reluctantly informed Karen that the body of the dog would have been dumped, along with all other waste, at the local land fill site. He said he could give her the number if she liked. She replied, rather sharply, that she would like! He passed her the number.

Karen dialled the number she had been given and seemed to wait an eternity before it was answered. Again, the male who responded was not very helpful until Karen threatened to come over and lock him up for obstructing the police. That seemed to focus his mind and he listened intently as she told him the problem. He asked politely when the body was reported. He then proceeded to explain that it would have been deposited in section 3A which was nearing capacity and would be filled in later that day.

"That cannot happen," said Karen." We need to examine that carcass. Is there any way you can hold off filling it in?"

"Well, it's most unusual," replied the man. "My boss will need to give the OK."

By now Karen was beginning to run on a short fuse. "Listen sir, get on the phone to your boss now and get that filling in stopped. Then get a gang of men down there ready to begin looking for that bloody dog. I'll be there in half an hour. Do you understand?"

"Yes," replied the man, meekly.

"Thank you," said Karen and slammed down the phone.

"Everything all right?" asked Alan Stanton.

"If you mean wading through tons of shit and waste to find a dead dog then yes, everything's bloody marvellous!"

"Sorry I asked," replied Alan.

Karen sighed. "Sorry Al," she said, "I'm a bit uptight at the moment."

"Apology accepted, if you need to talk about it, you know where I am," Alan replied.

"Thanks. I'll bear that in mind," Karen said. *That would be good*, she thought, *discussing the reason for my irritability, ie. shagging the boss, with anyone on the team.*

"Get a grip girl" she said under her breath. "I'm off to the local tip Al, see you later."

"Have fun," replied the office manager and returned to his paperwork.

Chapter 23

Pete had been called into the Superintendent's office to give his boss an update. Adrian Fowler was a high-flyer. He had only been a member of the police service for ten years but had already reached the rank of senior officer. He had been fast tracked via to the accelerated promotion courses operated by all British police forces. The superintendent's main priority was finance. He had a favourite saying 'NEVER SPEND A POUND WHEN A PENNY WILL DO.'

How the hell you are supposed to run major incident enquiries working to those constraints Pete would never know. He did, however, toe the party line whenever it was possible. Having a good office manager like Alan Stanton helped keep the books balanced. He returned to the incident room after giving the superintendent his briefing with his boss's words of, "Keep your eye on the overtime Peter," ringing in his ears.

"How did it go boss?" Alan asked, as Pete slumped down into a chair.

"Fucking great." He said, "he couldn't give a toss about the job as long as we keep the purse strings as tight as a duck's arse. Do you know, I never even got a cup of tea!"

"Is that a hint?" Alan chuckled.

"Would you mind, mate? White, no sugar thanks," Pete

asked, stretching his arms over his head to try to loosen some of the knots forming there.

Alan had picked up on Pete's tension. "Is everything OK, boss?"

"Yes thanks, Al. I'm just a bit uptight. We need a break in this flaming case."

"Everyone's feeling the strain today," said Alan. "Karen all but took my head off earlier."

"Really," replied Pete. "Wonder what's bugging her?" *As if I don't I know*, he thought!

"Probably the same as you," Alan said without looking at Pete." She thinks we're due something to develop in the enquiry as well." He handed Pete his cup of tea and returned to his figures.

The door burst open and Bill and Dave entered the office. "Is that a fresh brew, Al?" Bill asked.

"Yes, there's still some left in the pot," replied Alan.

"Oh, great thanks, mate. Do you want one Dave?"

"Yes please, white, three sugars."

"Blimey, no wonder you're a fat bastard," laughed Bill, as he poured out a second cup.

"Did you get anything from Wilkinson's address, Bill?" Pete asked.

"Well, his mother flaked out on us and we had to send her to hospital. Uniform are with her, and if she's up to it, they'll take her to ID the body. We had a good look around the house and especially his room. Clean as a whistle really, nothing helpful there at all. We confiscated his computer and it's with the tech. support people now."

"Good. let's hope they come up with something. We're not making much progress at the moment," sighed Pete.

Chapter 24

Michael lay awake, a thin film of sweat sitting on his furrowed brow. His eyes were wide open staring aimlessly into the darkness. The duvet had been kicked off as he tried to cool his fevered body. His mind was racing. *Fuck, fuck, fuck?* he thought. *How did they find it? It was buried deep enough. Maybe it was just bad luck. Yes,* he thought, *it was just bad luck.*

"We need to be more careful," he said.

"What do you mean," was the reply.

"We need to be more careful because they've found one of the bodies."

"How do you know?"

"I got a tissue sample to test. It had been sent by the pathology laboratory. It came from a body found in Brumby Woods. They wanted a full toxicology scan done on it. It was pure luck Darren gave it to me to do. Anybody else and they would know about the Curare."

"Did you destroy the results?"

"Yes."

"Well, that's all right then. You worry too much."

"One of us has to. You don't give a fuck what might

happen. It will be me who has to take all the blame if we're discovered."

"Relax. They'll never figure it out. There's nothing to connect us to the body. I got rid of his personal effects and dumped the car at the airport long stay car park. It will be months before the airport security find it and do some checks. Now go to sleep."

Michael rolled over and tried again to sleep. He fell into a dream filled sleep, all dogs and graves, until the persistent buzzing of his radio alarm told him it was time to get up. He would have normally jumped out of bed and commenced his early morning fitness regime; a hundred push ups, followed by a hundred pull ups and then a four-mile run. *Not this morning*, he thought. *I'm too tired.* He pulled the cover back over himself and tried to doze off.

After thirty minutes he had given up any hope of falling back to sleep. He rose, stripped naked, and showered. A light breakfast and he would be on his way to work, f*or another eight hours of riotous fun! as Darren would say*, he thought. "What a twat!" he said out loud.

He dressed, got into the car and headed for the lab, praying there would be no more surprises waiting for him today.

Chapter 25

Karen arrived at the landfill site. She knew, even from a few miles away, that she was close. She could see the large flocks of gulls circling overhead, swooping down randomly to land on the piles of rotting waste trying to scavenge a meal. The smell was the other giveaway and she quickly closed the car window. She drove through the gates, over to the quagmire that was the car park, and switched off the engine. Despite the fact that the windows were shut, she could smell the place. A rank mixture of disinfectant and mouldy vegetation invaded her nostrils. She opened her bag, took out her perfume, and sprayed a tissue with it. Holding this close to her nose she went round to the boot of the car and took out an old pair of walking shoes. Donning the thick socks that had been stuffed inside them she put on the shoes, she tucked the bottoms of her suit trousers inside the socks to keep them clean. "Better to feel a pratt rather than to get covered in shit and look one," she said to the scruffy-looking man who stood waiting for her at the bottom of the steps that led down from the site office.

"I'm Dan Wilson, site foreman, er, sorry it's so mucky but everything gets churned up by the lorries see, and what with the bad weather and all." The sentence tailed off as Karen ignored it and asked.

"Right, where's the site with the dog in it?"

"It's this way Miss"

Karen looked daggers at the man. Her pet hate was to be called 'Miss' It always sounded to her like she was a sixty-year-old spinster with a grey bun and a cat. She trudged after the man, dodging the puddles of stinking water on the way, taking care not to slip. The last thing she wanted was to fall on her arse in front of these men and make a laughing stock of herself. Walking between two large earth moving vehicles the man led her towards a huge crater in the ground. At the edge of the hole stood three men, leaning on shovels, waiting for them to arrive. Karen caught Wilson up as they arrive at the other group.

Wilson gathered the three other men to him and said, "OK lads. This lady is with the police and she wants us to find the body of a dog which was brought in a couple of days ago by one of our road crews. It should be easy to find. It will be in one of those yellow bags we use to dispose of dead animals, and they won't have thrown it in too far, so concentrate around the edges."

The men split up and commenced searching around the perimeter of the hole. Karen was amazed that they seemed unconcerned at the request. *I suppose you get used to working anywhere after a while*, she thought.

"We can wait in the office if you'd like? It's a bit warmer in there and the kettle will have nearly boiled. The lads will bring us the dog when they find it," said Wilson. Regretting her earlier coldness, Karen accepted the invitation gracefully and set off back through the dirt following closely behind the foreman.

The tea was delicious and the man produced a packet of Karen's favourite chocolate digestive biscuits. She had only just bitten into her third biscuit when there was a knock at the door. Dan Wilson went to answer it. He stepped outside, closing the door behind him to keep the warmth in. Karen could hear the rustling of plastic and the sound of retching as the bag was opened.

"My god, what a stench," said a voice.

"Yes, it's a bit ripe, isn't it," replied Wilson. "Fasten it up again please Joe."

The man twisted the top of the sack closed and secured it with a security tag. "Shall I put it inside another bag?" he asked Gary.

"Good idea, Joe. It will keep the stench in. I wouldn't like that smell inside my car."

Karen smiled to herself at the thoughtfulness of the last remark she had overheard. Wilson returned inside the office. "They've found it," he said. "Joe has taken it to your car and put it in the boot. Did you know you had left it unlocked, officer?"

Karen cringed at the remark but grinned when she realised that Dan was teasing her. "Thanks Dan. I knew the car would be safe here," she said.

"Yes, correct," he replied. "I'll see you off the premises officer."

Wilson was as good as his word and escorted Karen to her car. He even supported her by the arm as she struggled to take off her filthy walking shoes without putting her feet down. Finally, wearing her smart court shoes and with the cargo safely stashed in the boot, Karen drove off. She headed for the Talbot Animal Sanctuary where the cause of the dog's death would be established. The owner of the sanctuary, Phillip Talbot, had assisted the police in the past with animal related problems. He was an exceptional veterinary surgeon, choosing to treat animals in his charitable sanctuary rather than at a lucrative private practice. The fees he charged the police were always very reasonable. This helped keep expenses down during major enquiries like this one. *The Super would be pleased to hear that*, she thought.

When Karen arrived at the sanctuary, Phillip Talbot greeted her. He was small with a stocky build, he was dressed in a smart suit and Karen briefly realised that he was quite an attractive-looking man. *Steady tiger*, she thought to herself, *you're spoken for I wish!* He was already aware of what was required, having been briefed by Karen over the telephone from the refuse site office. He instructed two of his assistants to remove the dog from Karen's car and take it into his surgery.

"It will probably take a couple of days to do the tests," he told Karen. "I'll ring you with my initial findings results and follow that up with a full written report. I know you like everything in writing."

"Thanks Phillip," replied Karen. "Send your bill to Alan Stanton at the major incident room. He'll take care of it for you."

"Will do," Phillip said as he waved Karen off.

Chapter 26

Pete Bridle sat at the front of the room waiting to start the daily briefing. He knew that things were not moving as quickly as he might hope but he was experienced enough to know that this type of enquiry could not be rushed. Unless they were extremely lucky, and someone walked through the door and confessed to the murder, they would have to do it the long way. Slow though it might be, the standard, well established practices of police investigation would eventually bear fruit. He swept the room slowly through half-closed eyes. His gaze lingered briefly on Karen who was sitting, head down, facing her computer screen. The rest of the team were spread out across the room, chatting or checking their notes.

"Good morning, everyone," Pete said. "Can we make a start please?" The sound of chairs scraping across the floor followed his request as the team gave him their full attention. "Can we go around the room, one at a time please, briefly update us where you all are. Bill, would you start."

"Yes sir," replied Bill, shuffling up straight in his chair. "Well, we visited the home of the dead man and spoke briefly to his mother. She was shocked, obviously, and ended up being taken to the hospital for a check-up. She came through that OK and was escorted to the mortuary where she formally identified the man as her son Clive Wilkinson. We've arranged to interview her later this morning. The search of the house proved fruitless really. The man's room was all very orderly and bare, very few personal possessions apart from clothes, at all. His mother gave us permission to take his computer and it is with the technical support unit now. We also found details of his car. Unfortunately, it was not circulated on the PNC when he was reported missing, so we have no idea where it is. I've done that now so let's see if it turns up."

"Did they give you any idea how long it might be before the Technical boys had something for us," asked an officer from across the room.

"How long's a piece of string?" Bill replied, raising his palms face up in the air.

"Karen, you next please," ordered Pete. Karen swung around in her seat to face the rest of the team.

"As you all know I've been looking at the 'dog angle' in the case. I located the body of the dog that was buried on top of Clive Wilkinson and had it recovered for examination. I had a hunch it might be useful if we knew how it had died. I've also been checking through our systems for reports of any large dogs that have gone missing. I am trying to tie those up with any further reports of dogs found buried in remote locations. I'll update you when I've done some more digging! Sorry, no pun intended," said Karen, in response to the groans that echoed around the room.

"Do you need any help with that?" Pete asked Karen.

"I wouldn't mind. There will be a lot of leg work in this judging by the number of reports I have to follow up on."

"OK. Andy, can you double up with Karen please?" Pete

asked DC Andy Bower.

"Yes boss," replied Andy Bower.

Karen liked working alongside all the team but she especially enjoyed Andy, 'Battered', Bower's style of policing. He was rough and tough, good in a tight corner, but very thorough. It was rumoured that when he was a young constable he was sent to a report of a disturbance in a fish and chip shop in the village where he was the local bobby. When he arrived at the scene, he radioed his initial report back as, 'a large group of males inside the shop, threatening two of the female staff'. When he was asked by his controller if he needed any back up, he replied," No thank you, it's only some of the local lads playing up. I'll soon sort it out."

The next radio message Andy transmitted was a request for an ambulance to collect three youths with minor injuries. From witness reports, taken later by Andy's sergeant, it was stated that Andy had entered the shop, locked the door and, 'offered the youths two choices'. They picked the wrong one and paid the penalty. None of the youths made any complaint about Andy and it was rumoured that, after that, he only had to pass the shop and he would be waved down and a parcel of steaming fish and chips would be thrust through the car window. That's how Andy Bower got the nick name 'Battered'. Karen always smiled when she recalled that story. Andy, however, would only say that the lads slipped on the greasy shop floor when he asked them to leave!

Authors Note… this was a true incident only the names have been changed. I knew the officer concerned personally.

Chapter 27

Karen and Andy toiled for hours on their computers. They trawled through every recorded incident of large dogs found buried in remote locations. They then attempted to cross reference these with reports of missing dogs. Finally, they then looked to see if any of the addresses where the dogs were reported missing from were close to the locations of any of the buried dogs. Despite all their efforts there appeared to be nothing to link any of the locations to each other.

"Looks like we've drawn a blank here, Andy," said Karen switching off her computer with a bang.

"Afraid so," replied Andy. "I don't think it would do any harm if we visited some of the addresses where the dogs were reported missing from. I did notice that three of them had gone from scrap yards. That might be a link."

"Nothing to lose," Karen said, pulling her coat from the back of her chair and heading for the door.

"I'll get the addresses then, shall I?" Andy said, as Karen disappeared through the door. He raised his eyebrows as he looked at Alan Stanton, pressed the print key on his computer to obtain a list of the missing dogs, grabbed the copy, and rushed after Karen.

Karen was waiting in the car park, engine running. Andy

hadn't even got his seat belt on before Karen had pulled out of her parking spot, turned sharp left, and joined the traffic on the busy road outside the station. "OK. Which way are we going?"

"Right," said Andy, with a wicked gleam in his eye.

"What, right?" Karen asked.

"Yes," replied Andy.

"Oh, bloody hell!" Karen shrieked, as she tried to find a gap in the traffic to allow her to turn around. "You might have told me before I pulled out of the yard."

"Chance would have been a fine thing," chuckled Andy.

"Sorry, Andy. I'm a bit edgy today. Where do I need to go?"

"Head out towards Bradley, the first address is there."

Karen drove towards Bradley, careful to follow every direction Andy gave her. They eventually arrived at the address, a scruffy looking salvage yard surrounded by a high chain link fence. Karen parked outside gates on the dirty track road. Entering the yard, they headed towards a rundown hut with the word 'office' painted on the door. When they were about halfway across the yard, they both stopped in their tracks as a snarling dog rushed out from behind a scrap car and charged towards them. The dog came to an abrupt halt as it reached the end of the stout chain that tethered it. Straining at the leash it remained stationery, barking and growling at the two anxious police officers who stood motionless only inches away. The office door opened. A large male appeared at the door, a half-smoked cigarette dangling from his mouth. He threw a rusty piece of metal in the direction of the dog. "Shut up you noisy bastard, get back in that car," he yelled. The dog turned and skulked back behind the rusting vehicle. "What do you two want?" he asked, in the same manner he had used to the dog.

"Mr Broady?" Karen asked.

"Who wants to know?" the man replied.

"I do," replied Andy, advancing towards the man whilst reaching inside his coat for his Warrant Card.

"Coppers! Huh, I thought you didn't look like one of my regular clientele, someone who needed a wheel bearing for a 1994 Ford Transit."

No, thought Andy, *we've got all our own teeth and aren't covered in fucking tattoos!*

"What do you want here anyway?" growled the man.

"Shall we go into the office? We need to ask you a few questions," said Karen sweetly, brushing past the man.

"Just a minute, you can't just barge in there. You need a search warrant."

"Why, have you got something to hide?" Andy asked as he too entered the office.

Karen knew that the police were often viewed with suspicion by the owners of these types of businesses who often walk the narrow line between honest work and very dodgy practices. Not all however were crooks, many were people who often helped the police with stolen vehicles and gangs of 'vehicle ringers'. Mr Broady however, judging by his attitude, fell into the first of the two categories. The owner followed them into the office and quickly sat down. He visibly relaxed once the desk was between himself and Andy Bower. Andy had taken up a position in front of the door and glared down at Broady menacingly.

"Now Mr Broady, I understand you reported your guard dog missing," said Karen. She too remained standing as the only free chair didn't look fit for human occupation.

"Christ, that was years ago, don't tell me you've found old Rocky? And here's me thinking coppers were useless. Well, I don't want it back, thank you. I've got another one now. Oh, but you know that, you've met him, haven't you?" Broady said laughing, then nearly collapsing with fits of bronchial coughing.

Ignoring the choking man, Karen asked, "What happened to Rocky?"

The man eventually managed to get his coughing under control and, through a filthy handkerchief, replied. "I assume it was let out by the bastards that tried to rob this place. They forced the gate open so I reckon the dog got out then."

"You didn't mention the place had been burgled when you reported the dog missing."

"I didn't think it was worth it. They tried to force the door, but it was too strong, so they never got in. Nothing was taken from the yard so, what was the point?"

"It was a big dog wasn't it. Did they cut its chain?"

"Yes, Rocky was big, vicious too. They had no need to cut his chain, the dog roamed around the yard unleashed on a night. I often wonder if he managed to bite them before he escaped, though, like I said he was a nasty bastard. Bit me a few times."

"Thank you for your cooperation, Mr Broady," said Karen.

"Anytime darling, are you sure you won't stay for a drink?"

"Don't push it arsehole," said Andy as he opened the door for Karen and him to leave.

"What a tosser," said Andy, neatly sidestepping a large pile of dog excrement.

They returned to the car and continued onto the next address. This turned out to be a private house and the owner was still very upset about his missing pet, despite the fact it was nearly two years since it had disappeared. The animal was a pedigree male German Shepherd very valuable, having twice won the local dog show. The owner suspected that it had been stolen by a rival breeder who had either killed it or was secretly breeding from it. He couldn't understand how the dog had been taken from the shed where it was kept without the dog making any noise. He also informed them that there had been no sign of a forced entry on the shed door. The owner did admit however, that he was forgetful and might have put the dog away without locking the shed. The two police officers took their leave and headed for the other addresses.

They returned to the incident room later that day, after checking seven possible leads. They were enjoying a sandwich and a coffee when Bill Hodge returned to the office and asked how they had got on. "Nothing, a complete blank," Karen replied.

"Mind if I have a look?" Bill asked.

"Help yourself," replied Karen as she passed him the seven reports they had looked at. Bill took them over to his desk to examine them. This was how the team worked. Sometimes in a complicated and involved investigation like this one, officers could get 'too close' to the task they were assigned to.

After about half an hour Bill called Andy and Karen over to his desk. "Grab a chair, guys, I think I might have found something." Bill began to explain his theory to the other two. "A couple of things seem to jump out at me," said Bill. "Firstly, I noticed that four of the missing dogs came from scrap yards.

One of the owners, a Mr Broady, stated that there had been an attempt to gain entry to the yard office, but he didn't report it because they didn't get in. Did any of the other yard owners mention an attempted burglary?"

"To be honest Bill, we never asked, most of them weren't very helpful anyway," replied Karen.

"OK, secondly," continued Bill, "at the private addresses where the family pets were taken, all the owners were mystified as to how the dogs had been taken or released, without any noise. In two of the cases the garages or sheds where the dogs were kept were broken into but nothing was stolen. What does that seem to indicate?" asked Bill.

Karen and Andy's faces both lit up at the same time. "Are we saying that someone stole these dogs and tried to disguise the fact by making it look like they escaped as a result of another crime? But why would they do that?"

"We all know what was found on top of Clive Wilkinson don't we?" Bill asked.

"Yes, a large dog. Oh Christ," said Karen. "You don't think there may be more bodies buried where some of those other dogs were found do you?"

"Could be, but before we start digging up the whole of the county, we need get onto those other scrap yards. We need to know if they were also subjected to an attempted burglary at the time their dogs were reported missing. If you have any trouble with them, lock them up for obstructing the police. I'll update the boss when I get home. OK, get on with it. I'll see you in the morning at the daily briefing. I hope I'm wrong about this but, if I'm not, then we've got big trouble."

Chapter 28

Pete was not fully asleep when his phone rang on the bed side table. He was in that peaceful twilight zone that enveloped you after you had made long, slow, love to a beautiful woman. He stretched out carefully across Karen's still body, noticing a small glistening patch of perspiration that had settled between her breasts. He picked up his phone and answered with a brief, "Hello."

"Hello boss, it's Bill."

"Yes Bill, what can I do for you?"

"I just wanted to fill you in before the briefing in the morning. We may have a bigger problem than we first thought."

"Why do I get the feeling I'm not going to like this, Bill? Give it to me then"

Bill proceeded to relay the information to Pete and explain the theory that the team members had come up with. Pete listened patiently thinking how difficult it was to listen to what Bill was saying having already heard it from Karen. Bill finished talking and waited, silently allowing Pete to digest what he had just told him.

"Thanks Bill. I'll think on it overnight. We'll discuss it at the briefing in the morning, bye."

Pete switched off the phone. Karen had opened her eyes and was propped up on one arm looking at him.

"Was that Bill giving you the news?" she asked.

"Yes," replied Pete. "If what you two have figured out is true we've got a massive problem facing us." Pete started chuckling.

"What's so funny?" Karen asked.

"I was just picturing the superintendent's face when I tell him how much more money and manpower I'll need. Bet I don't get a cup of tea off him."

Karen reached up and tried to pull him down towards her. Pete resisted, glancing at his watch.

"Sorry babe," he said, but before he could finish what he was going to say, Karen said. "Yes, I know. You've got to go."

"You know I don't want to but I've no alternative. The child minder leaves at eight thirty and it's a quarter past already. I'll see you in the morning." With that he slipped from the warm bed, dressed and left after giving Karen a soft kiss on the lips. Karen turned over and buried her head beneath the pillows.

As Pete drove home, he thought about how the situation with the case would change drastically if Bill and Karen's theory was correct. *Bloody hell*, he thought to himself, *what a crock of shit this could turn out to be!* He increased the volume on the car CD player and let his mind drift away, soothed by the gentle sound of Mozart.

Chapter 29

Pete called the briefing to order. Everyone settled down, clutching cups of tea or coffee, and waited for the boss to start. He called Bill first. Bill explained to the rest of the team what Karen and Andy had done and what conclusions they had come to. The room remained deadly quiet as each person absorbed the information and began to realise the implications. This could make their investigations massive. No one spoke.

"OK," said Pete. "First job is to get round those remaining scrap yards and find out if any of them were screwed." Pete acknowledged Bill as he put his hand up.

"That's covered boss, Karen and Andy will do it. They've been instructed not to take any crap off the owners. If they don't cooperate, they're to lock them up and bring them in."

"Thanks, Bill," replied Pete. "Now whilst I go and break the good news to our beloved leader, we need to chase up the technical support boys, and check with the command centre to see if there is any Operational Support Section on duty. If we have to start digging, we're going to need their help. Right, everybody know what they're doing? Good, let's get to it!"

The meeting broke up. Each individual member either reached for a desk phone or pulled on a coat as they left the office. Pete took the time to have a quick word with the office manager and obtain an update on the budget before heading off to see the superintendent.

"My God, Inspector, are you sure about all this?" the superintendent asked.

"The theory is good sir," replied Pete. "It will depend on the answers we get from the other scrap yard owners. If they turn out like we think they will, we will have to dig up one of the sites where a dead dog was found. If there is anything there, like a human body, then it's a strong possibility that there will be bodies at the other locations as well."

"How many are we looking at?" the superintendent asked, ashen faced.

"Possibly seven,"

"Hell, Pete! It doesn't bear thinking about. The manpower implications will be horrendous. This could blow the divisional budget out of the water. Still, nothing we can do about it. Get what resources you need to deal with this if it escalates. I'll let the divisional commander know. I hope he's got deep pockets. Would you like a cup of tea before you go?"

"No thank you sir. I better get on."

"Right oh, Peter. Keep me updated."

Pete closed the door behind him and winked at the superintendent's middle-aged secretary on the way past.

"He offered me a cup of tea," he said to her, laughing.

The secretary looked at him as if he was stupid and returned to her work.

Chapter 30

When Pete returned to the incident room there was a note on his desk asking him to contact the technical support unit.

"Did you take this message, Al?"

"Yes, it came in about half an hour ago. How did it go with the superintendent?"

"Remarkably well all things considering. He gave me the go ahead for extra manpower, with the usual advice on money of course. Guess what the most remarkable thing was though?"

"He offered you a cup of tea," replied Alan.

"How the fuck did you know that?" asked Pete in amazement. By way of an answer Alan just tapped his finger on the side of his nose.

"Clever bastard," said Pete with a grin. "I'm off to see what the tech guys have found. If anyone needs me, I have my mobile with me."

"Right ho, Pete."

Peter left the Incident Room and made his way out of the building and across the yard to where the technical support unit was based. He waited patiently outside the door for someone to answer the intercom. This was probably one of the most secure sections in the force, along with Special Branch and the drug squad office. A voice asked for his identity and, after confirming it, the automatic door opened allowing Pete to enter. He made his way along a small corridor to a door marked Computer Section. He knocked once. The door opened and Peter was invited to enter by a small, rotund man, dressed in a brown dust coat. His hair was thinning at the top with streaks of grey at the temple. A pair of thick rimmed glasses perched delicately on his nose. He smelt faintly of cigarette smoke.

"Welcome to the dingy world of the TSU. Long-time no see, Peter. How have you been? How's Jenny." The technician who had admitted Pete was called George Blake. He and Peter had been friends for a number of years. George had left a promising career as a computer analyst with a local pharmaceutical company to help set up the TSU in the days before technology began to impact so greatly on police work. It was an astute move at the time by the then chief constable Tony Burke. Burke had recognised that the police needed to keep abreast of anything involving computers, surveillance or communications. His foresight had earned him the exalted position at the home office, of Her Majesties Inspector of Constabulary with Special Responsibility for Technical Issues. Burke had chosen the right man to set up and run the TSU. George Blake had tackled the task with energy and enthusiasm and within a year he had established a very well-staffed, efficient unit that had progressed to where it was today, the envy of most other forces.

"I'm fine thanks, George. Jenny has her ups and downs though as you can imagine."

"Yes, it can't be easy for either of you, please give her mine and Jean's best wishes when you see her," said George. "Now, I have something interesting to show you regarding the

Wilkinson case."

George led Pete over to his desk and handed him a blue manila folder. "It's all in there, times, dates, sites etc. Is there a sexual angle to this case?"

"Possibly," replied Pete. "Why do you ask?"

"Well, our chum Wilkinson seemed to like some particularly interesting internet sites," said George, taking off his glasses and wiping them on his dustcoat. "Like I said, they are all listed in the report, but briefly, he was into S&M. Some of the sites he visited are pretty extreme. I also managed to get into his email account. Fairly mundane stuff mostly but a couple of the messages seem to indicate he may have taken an active part in some sexual encounters. I'll leave that one for you and your team to look into."

"Thanks, George, as usual a great job. Appreciate the help."

"It was my pleasure. Take care of yourself and the family."

"Will do," Pete said and made his way back to his office.

Chapter 31

Karen and Andy sat silently in the car outside the last scrap yard on their list. They were both trying to come to terms with what they had uncovered. All but two of the vehicle dismantlers had informed them that their offices had been attacked at the time their guard dogs had gone missing, but that nothing appeared to have been stolen. They had all neglected to mention this fact when they made their initial report. Most of these less reputable scrap yard owners were anti- police and didn't want anyone looking into a minor crime just in case something more serious was uncovered! Karen rubbed her eyes and sighed. "You know what this means don't you Andy?"

"Yep," came his clipped reply. "It means we may have another seven bodies on our hands if it turns out the missing dogs were buried on top of humans."

"The boss is going to love this. Let's get back to the office and break the good news to him," said Karen, starting the car and spinning the front wheels as she accelerated away.

Just as Karen joined the main ring road her mobile rang. She clicked the telephones hands free button on the steering wheel and answered, "DC James."

"Hello, Karen, this is Phillip Talbot at the animal sanctuary."

"Hi, Phillip. I'm assuming you have some news on the dog for me."

"Yes, I have. We found large traces of ethylene glycol in the body of the dog. It was poisoned."

"What on earth is ethylene glycol and where do you get it from?" asked Karen.

"Well, it's very easy to obtain, in fact, I bet you have some at home in your garage," replied Talbot. "It's the main constituent of motor engine antifreeze!"

"Christ," said Karen. "That's a bit unusual, isn't it?"

"Actually. I'm afraid it's not," replied Talbot. "It's the easiest way to kill a dog. Unscrupulous dog breeders have used it on competitor's animals for years. The amazing thing is that dogs are so attracted to it you don't have to force them to drink it. I've known cases where dogs were still gulping it down as they died."

"Apart from the dog breeders you mentioned, who else would know about this?"

"Anyone could. If you wanted to get rid of a dog, all you would need to do was to look up 'The Best Way To Kill A Dog,' on the internet. It's all there for you."

"Thanks, Phillip, will you send me the full report please?"

"Already on the way," replied Phillip. "We must go out for a drink sometime. Shall I ring you?"

"That would be nice, as long as it's not ethylene glycol, but I think I'll be rather busy for the foreseeable future. Let me get back to you."

"Don't leave it too long now," said Phillip and the phone went dead. Blushing, Karen turned to look at Andy who had heard the full conversation on the speaker. "You say a word about that and you're a dead man Bower."

"My lips are sealed," replied Andy and gave Karen a look that said butter would not melt in his mouth.

Chapter 32

When Karen and Andy arrived back at the major incident room, Pete and Bill were studying a thick report that was open on Pete's desk. Judging by the dark expressions on their faces they weren't trying to pick out the winner of the three thirty race, at Kempton. As Karen approached the desk, she heard Bill say, "He seems to have been into some fairly heavy stuff. I'll have a word with Vice, see if they've come across any of these internet sites."

"Good idea, Bill, but first let's look more closely at his emails, I'm sure there's something in there for us. Oh, hi, you two, any news?" said Pete as he looked up at Karen and Andy.

"Yes, and it's all bad," sighed Karen.

Bill and Pete immediately stopped what they were doing and gave Karen their full attention. She slumped down into a chair and began her report. "Five out of the seven scrap yard owners we visited failed to mention that there had been an attempt to burgle the office at the same time they reported their guard dogs missing. That information led us to think that we may have the beginnings of some type of MO. We must now assume the burglaries were used as a smoke screen to hide the fact that it was the dogs the perpetrator was really after. If that is the case then we have to assume that the dogs were taken to use as cover for other crimes, i.e., murder, seven in all, plus Clive Wilkinson. I've also had a verbal report on how the dog found at Wilkinson's burial site was killed. It was poisoned using ordinary antifreeze."

"Antifreeze?" asked Bill, slightly surprised.

"Yes, apparently dogs can't get enough of it. You don't have to force it down them and of course it's easily obtained. We'd never be able to trace everyone who bought it. Hell, I got some myself last week."

The room stayed silent for what seemed like an eternity after Karen had finished speaking. Everyone was trying to come to terms with what Karen's report could mean, they could be dealing with more than one murder! Pete realised that they now needed to check all the other sites where dogs' remains had been found. If Karen's conclusions were correct, then a further seven bodies would be discovered.

"Good work, you two," said Pete. His head was spinning. "What to do first?" he asked himself. "Bill, get onto the command centre, confirm with the force duty officer if there are any Operational Support Groups (OSS) on duty first thing in the morning. If there are, ask him to get the OSS sergeant to ring me urgently. Also ask if he will contact the force medical officer and arrange for sufficient doctors to be available for 0800 hours tomorrow to attend the burial sites. Tell him a list of the locations will be sent through later today. Karen, can you prepare that list please as soon as you can? Andy, make sure we have all team members here at 0600 hours, I want one of our team to attend each of the locations along with the OSS groups. Alan, could you get onto SOCO, explain the situation. They'll have to call out more officers for early turn, one officer will be needed at each site to avoid cross contamination, explain overtime will be paid. Anyone think of anything else?"

"What about the report from the technical support unit?" Bill asked.

"We'll leave that for now. We've enough on our plates at the moment. OK everyone got a job?" There was a murmured yes in reply. "Good, let's get to it then, I want everything in place by this afternoon."

The team dispersed, each too busy with their tasks to think about what was to come. Peter Bridle put everyone's thoughts into perspective as he half whispered, "God help us all with this one!"

Peter's next tasks would be to quickly brief the superintendent and then visit the press liaison officer to update them and call a press conference if the superintendent thought it necessary. It was usually prudent to give the news hounds an early look at the situation in order to control what was released and prevent any wild guesses as to what was going on. He reached for the telephone and dialled the superintendent's number.

After briefing Superintendent Fowler, it was agreed to go ahead with a short press conference, confirming the suspicious death of Wilkinson but not to mention the possible link to more murders. Pete made his way to the media office at Force Headquarters. Two hours later he had agreed a statement with the on duty media officer, Maggie Hebden, and a press conference was to be called for two o'clock that afternoon. Peter was not looking forward to it one bit. He always felt as if he had been fed to the sharks when he took part in one. Still, it had to be done, "force policy and all that," as the superintendent would say.

Chapter 33

The media conference room was filling up quickly and becoming hot and stuffy as representatives from all the local and national television, radio and newspapers filed in. The word had got out that there was a big story about to break here and they were all determined to be the first with the critical probing question that might blow the case wide open. The room went silent as Peter, Maggie Hebden, the media liaison officer, and Superintendent Fowler entered the room and made their way to the rostrum. Maggie sat between the two police officers and waited until the room settled down. She looked around slowly, recognising the odd face here and there from her days as a reporter with the local radio station and, later, as chief crime correspondent of the Daily Echo. She knew exactly how this conference would go. She would take the lead and read out the statement that she and Peter Bridle had prepared earlier. Everyone in the room had been issued with a copy so they were familiar with its contents. She would then throw the meeting open to questions that Peter Bridle would be expected to answer. Adrian Fowler was there as 'the face of senior police management' and would probably not have to say anything. Coughing gently to clear her throat and gain attention, she commenced her statement.

"As you are no doubt aware the police were called to a location in Brumby Woods four days ago where a body was discovered. The body was that of a white male, approximately forty to forty-five years old. The male has been identified as Clive Wilkinson, a local man from the grange estate area, who had been reported missing around the estimated time of his death. The autopsy showed that Mr Wilkinson had been dead for about three weeks. Cause of death was due to asphyxiation. Relatives have been informed. The police are treating his death as 'suspicious.' Detective Inspector Peter Bridle is leading the enquiry and he will try to answer any questions you may have. Now who's first please?"

A sea of hands immediately waved from the floor, like a class of excited school children eager to answer their teacher's question. Maggie pointed to a small male with greasy hair and sharp features. He had a half-smoked cigarette tucked behind one ear and sniffed as he talked. The man stood and introduced himself. "Paul Adams — Barchester News. Detective Inspector, could you tell us the exact circumstances surrounding the discovery of the deceased?"

"Certainly," replied Peter, trying to keep the edge from his voice. "It was discovered by a member of the public whilst walking their dog. The dog unearthed some bones and they called us." Peter looked away immediately he had answered the question to prevent the man from asking anything else.

Maggie nodded at a female reporter who stood and spoke in a deep sultry voice, "Lisa Warcup — BBC News." Inspector, were there any signs of violence on the body. The cause of death is given as asphyxiation, was he strangled?"

Peter turned to meet her gaze, staring into her deep brown

eyes before answering. "We do not believe Mr Wilkinson was strangled; there were no marks around the neck to indicate any pressure had been applied to the wind pipe. The pathologist thinks some type of drug may have been administered but toxicology tests have revealed nothing. Obviously, that still remains a matter of great concern to us. The only other marks of any significance were on the wrists. The bruising there would seem to indicate that the man was secured before his death."

As the meeting continued Peter fielded a series of questions about the deceased, the next stages in the enquiry and the expected outcome of the case. Things were seemingly coming to a conclusion when, Paul Adams suddenly rose to his feet unannounced.

"Just one more point, Inspector, if I might?"

"We are just about to finish," interrupted Maggie. "The inspector is a very busy man."

"I completely understand that, but I'll only take a moment of his time."

"It's all right, Maggie, I'll take it," said Peter. "What is it you'd like to ask me, Mr Adams?"

"Can you tell us why you omitted to inform us that the bones found by the member of the public were from the corpse of a dog and that Wilkinson's body was, in actual fact, found buried beneath them? A strange manner in which to dispose of a murder victim do you not think Inspector? Oh, and is there any truth in the rumour that there may be more discoveries of this type?"

An excited buzz ran around the room as the other members of the press core picked up on this fact. *Why had it been kept from them?* they demanded to know.

"Where the fuck did he get that from?" whispered Peter angrily to Maggie Hebden.

Her face reddening as she stood up, Maggie tried to bring some semblance of order back to the meeting. The press would have none of it, hurling questions at the three bemused figures on the rostrum. It was finally left to Superintendent Fowler to bring the proceedings to a close by informing everyone that "There would be no further questions at this time but that a further statement would be released later if any more information became available."

Back at the Press Office Pete Bridle was blazing. "I'd love to know who told that little weasel about the burial site," he snarled.

"He's a good reporter," said Maggie. "He probably sniffed out a witness from the scene or he has a contact in the force that slips him information on the side."

"They'll be on their side if I ever find out who it was," said Pete. He realised suddenly that sounding off like this at Maggie would do no good. He needed her to fend off the media so he ate humble pie and apologised. Maggie accepted graciously and asked him to keep her updated with any developments. Promising he would, Pete left her office and made his way back to the MIR to see how the rest of the team were progressing.

Chapter 34

All members of the task force that Peter Bridle had assembled were gathered in the large briefing room at the Divisional HQ. Pete stood and asked for silence. He looked about at the officers and support staff spread out in front of him. It sometimes amazed him how a police force could at times struggle to get an officer to the scene of a burglary but when a serious incident arose manpower was never an issue. He sighed at the apparent lack of priorities that the police applied to their workloads. *Still,* he thought, *needs must when the devil calls!* He coughed to ensure everyone's attention.

"Ladies and gentlemen thank you for being so punctual and welcome to 'Operation Backlash'. As you are now aware every one of you has been assigned to a workgroup headed by a member of my incident team. Each group has a briefing file outlining their duties in this operation. It is vitally important that everything that is done at each site is fully recorded and documented. There will be additional uniform officers in attendance at all seven locations to deal with members of the media or public who will inevitably turn up. The media office is open and all enquiries concerning the operation should be directed at them. If and when, any human remains are discovered, once SOCO and the FMEs have finished with them, the command centre will arrange to have them recovered to the mortuary. We have several of our registered undertakers on standby to convey the deceased away. We will be operating on Force Radio Talk Group seventeen. I will be mobile between the locations and available by radio."

Just as it appeared to the people gathered in the room that Peter had finished talking, he took a deep breath and stared hard at everyone. "Most of you know me, if not personally, then by reputation. You know that I do not make idle threats, so listen very carefully to what I say." The sounds of shuffling echoed around the room as the people there seemed to sit up to attention. A silence followed.

"If I find out that anyone here says anything to anybody about what happens today then I'll have them disciplined and off the force. If it turns out, as we suspect it may, that we are dealing with multiple murders the last thing we need is the media crawling all over us whilst we try to find the offender. BE WARNED! Now good luck and off you go."

Pete stood and watched in silence as the teams dispersed, each destined for their own small section of hell he supposed. He turned as he felt a hand touch his arm.

"That last bit was rather on the strong side don't you think, Peter?"

Peter looked once again into the dark brown eyes that nestled behind the thick gold rimmed spectacles that belonged to Dr Amir Patel.

"We've already had one leak, Amir," replied Peter. "We can't afford this investigation to be compromised by any loose talk, not with what we suspect might be coming."

"I understand," said Amir. "Now, where are we going to

first?"

Amir, as the senior police surgeon, was to remain with Pete as his advisor. He was also available to give support to the other, less experienced, doctors who had been drafted in to help with the case.

"Have you got a pin?" Pete asked handing the list of locations to the doctor. Amir smiled.

"Let's just stay here and wait for the first call to come in from one of the sites."

"A sensible suggestion, as always, Doctor. I'm famished, fancy a coffee and a bacon sandwich," said Peter mischievously.

"Coffee would be fine," replied Amir, not responding to Peter's comment. They had been friends for long enough for Amir to understand Peter's humour and to take no offence from it.

Chapter 35

The canteen was nearly empty. Most of the staff who had breakfasted early were now gone, engaged on their normal daily duties. Pete and Amir sat silently near a window, Pete's radio receiver lying on the table between them hissing with static. Despite being hungry earlier, Pete had found his appetite had diminished and a half-eaten bacon sandwich lay discarded on his plate. His stomach was churning as he waited impatiently for the radio to spring into life with news of a find, he didn't have to wait long.

"Zero Nine to Zero One, a message over."

Pete snatched up the radio and pressed the transmit button. "Zero One receiving, go ahead," he replied.

"Zero One, WE HAVE A HIT!"

Pete stared anxiously at Amir and nodded. They both recognised the code words that indicated a body had been discovered. "Roger, en route," was Pete's tense reply.

Pete glanced at the list of locations that Karen had produced. Zero Nine group were at Kingsway Copse. He informed Amir. "It will take about twenty minutes to get there, let's go!" Both men rose from their seats and hastily made their way down to the car park where Pete had a marked police car and driver waiting. Before they even had time to fasten their seat belts, the driver had the car started and, with blue lights flashing and sirens wailing, was pulling out into the traffic on the main road.

"Do you know where we're going?" Pete asked the driver.

"Yes, Kingsway Copse, boss. I've been monitoring the radio," said the driver.

"Good man," replied Pete and settled down in the back seat to gather his thoughts.

As Pete had predicted, the journey to Kingsway Copse took twenty-two minutes. The driver stopped at the assembly point just outside the small wooded area that made up the copse. One of Pete's team was waiting to meet them and escort them to the scene. In a small clearing, they joined a group of officers standing around a large gaping hole. The officers who had been digging were resting on their shovels, red faced and breathless. A Scenes of Crime Officer (SOCO) and one of Amir's colleagues, dressed in the regulation white paper overalls, crouched in the hole. Pete and Amir approached thoughtfully and stood watching as the pair in white carefully scraped loose soil away to expose more of the gruesome find. After about ten minutes the two climbed carefully out of the hole and the SOCO. began taking a series of photographs. As he did Pete's radio sprang into life.

"Zero Four to Zero One, a message over."

With a trembling hand Pete hit the transmit button and responded. "Go Ahead Zero Four."

"Zero one from Zero Four. WE HAVE A HIT!"

"Roger. Let me know if you need me to attend."

"Roger will do. Zero Four out."

Pete looked towards Amir and mouthed silently, "another

one." His attention was then drawn back to the situation at hand and he listened intently as the police surgeon and SOCO officer gave him a brief update. Pete was informed that the body was a male, badly decomposed. Rough estimate of how long it had been there was at least a year. The autopsy would tell more. The only obvious sign of trauma was a broken wrist! Pete thanked the men for their report and left the scene to be dealt with by the group leader.

Pete and Amir made their way back to the waiting car. Pete checked the location of the second find, another remote wooded area. He decided to return to the incident room and wait for further updates. He broadcast the fact to all the groups and instructed the driver to take them back.

Over the next five hours all seven groups reported the message 'WE HAVE A HIT'.

Amir showed no signs of surprise or embarrassment when Pete uttered, "Oh, fucking hell," when the seventh report came in. Pete's worst fears were now realised. They had seven bodies. It looked like they were dealing with a mass murderer! He sat at his desk, head in his hands, his mind racing.

Chapter 36

When Pete's head had cleared a little, he began to come to terms with the reality of the situation he was dealing with. All the bodies had been recovered, SOCO were dealing with the scenes. Despite the numbness felt, Pete's body and mind slipped onto 'Auto-Pilot'. He reached for the radio handset and issued the stand down order for the operation staff. He then instructed all group leaders to meet at the MIR at 0900 hours the following day to debrief. The members of his team he ordered back to this office immediately. *Now the work really begins,* he thought.

Amir informed him that he would attend the mortuary the following morning to oversee the post-mortem examinations. Pete muttered his thanks as Amir took his leave. In dribs and drabs the team began to return to the office, exchanging gory details with each other whilst they hung around waiting for the boss to give them further orders. Pete's first instruction was to tell everyone to get a hot meal and a drink, he was conscious of the fact that some of the teams had been working for hours without a proper break. The last thing Pete wanted was for anyone to begin suffering from stress or fatigue. He was going to need everybody fit and well for the work that lay ahead. He made a mental note to contact the welfare department the next day. As the team left the office, Pete asked Bill Hodge to stay for a few minutes in order to have a quick word with him. Bill obliged and pulled his chair closer to Pete's desk.

"Do you want me to leave, boss?" asked Alan Stanton, the office manager.

"No, it's OK, Al, you must have lots to get on with."

Bill looked at his boss and asked. "What's on your mind, Pete?"

"What isn't?" came back Pete with a tired sigh. "I really just wanted to run some thoughts past you, see if you think I'm missing anything.

"Firstly, we need to identify all the bodies we have found and establish their addresses and what the causes of death are.

"Secondly, we need to check the names against our current list of missing persons going back say, eight to ten years.

"We need to identify their next of kin and inform them.

"We need to check out all the deceased's backgrounds, see if there are any similarities between them. You know the sort of thing I mean, hobbies, occupations, interests etc. If there are, we need to establish if there is a common link. There's still the data from Wilkinson's computer that needs analysing, I'd like you to do that first thing tomorrow, after the morning debrief, I'm sure there's a thousand other tasks, but I think that will do for starters. What do you think?"

"Sound's OK to me. I'll let you know if I come up with anything else," replied Bill.

"Thanks," said Pete. "Now go and get yourself something to eat, see you back here in an hour."

Pete watched as Bill left the office then picked up his desk telephone. He dialled the extension for the superintendent and gave him an update. The super was very supportive, yet again, and wished Pete luck. Next Pete dialled the PRO's extension and spoke to Maggie Hebden.

"It's as bad as you hoped it wouldn't be," she said.

"Yes, unfortunately it is. Could you cobble a press statement together? Enough to keep them off our backs until the post-mortems are done."

"No problem," said Maggie, "leave that with me,"

"Thanks, love. I'll talk to you later," Pete said, and replaced the phone on the receiver.

His mobile bleeped with a text message. He opened it. It was from Karen asking if they could meet. He replied saying it would be difficult, what with the late finish he would inevitably have that day and the fact he must see his family before they went to bed. He received no reply! "Bollocks," he growled.

"Did you say something, Pete?" asked Alan Stanton.

"Just thinking out loud, Al," he said.

The team began to drift back into the office. Pete's stomach growled and he realised he had been so busy thinking about everyone else's welfare he had forgotten his own. "Cheese and ham," said a voice as a paper bag plonked onto his desk. Pete looked up to see Karen's lovely face smiling down at him. "I knew you'd forget to get yourself something. Sorry," she whispered. Pete knew what she meant and thanked her.

Pete bit into his sandwich, chewed on it like it was cardboard then took a swig of coffee. He swallowed then prepared to issue his team with their orders.

Chapter 37

The following morning the office was nearly empty when Pete arrived. Bill was already crouched over his computer, checking the Wilkinson data. Alan Stanton was busy doing what office managers do. It was not long however before the team leaders from Operation Search arrived at the office. Pete called one of the CID secretaries in to take notes, once she had arrived, he commenced the debrief. Each team leader ran through their particular area of the operation. It seemed that most things had gone well, only a couple of the groups experiencing minor problems with press or members of the public. Pete thanked them for their assistance and pointed them in the direction of Alan so that they could sort out their group's overtime claims. The secretary left, promising to have the minutes typed up and on Pete's computer by that afternoon.

Pete wandered over to Bill's desk carrying two steaming cups of tea. "There you go, mate," he said. "Tea, same as you like your beer, flat, warm and weak."

"Like piss you mean?" Bill replied, smiling.

"Did I say that?" Pete responded. "Found anything useful yet?"

"I think I may have. As you know, Wilkinson was heavily

into S&M, not only as a voyeur, but also as a participant. It seems he made regular visits to an Internet site called 'Beautiful Dominants.' He made several appointments to visit them."

"How did he make the appointments?" asked Pete.

"By email," replied Bill.

"Any details on who he saw or when?"

"Yes, but he never saw the same one twice, seemed he liked a variety."

"When was the last time he visited someone?"

"Let's see, there's a message here from someone called Melinda, arranging a visit. It's from about six weeks ago."

"Did you think something could have gone wrong with that session?"

"It's possible I suppose. That could account for the marks on his wrist."

"Do we have an address?"

Bill scrolled through the message until he arrived at the information he was looking for. "Yes, it's here. He went to forty-seven Armstrong Terrace," he said, excitedly.

"Grab your coat, Bill."

"Why, where are we going?" he asked.

"We're going to check out that address. This might be the break we've been looking for."

Chapter 38

The weather had closed in, the heavy dark clouds that had promised rain now delivered. Bill sat in the passenger seat, a street map of the town spread out on his lap.

"Follow the ring road around to the Wellington Road Estate," he instructed Pete. "Once we get there, we take the third turning on the right, that should bring us into Massey Street, Armstrong Terrace is about half way down on the left."

"OK," replied Pete," that's not the most salubrious area in town, is it?"

"No, it's bloody awful now, although when I was a kid, it was quite posh."

Peter drove steadily through the light traffic. His mind was spinning with anticipation at what they might find. Could this really give them the break they so desperately needed to crack open this now major case?

"Only about another mile or so, boss, before we turn off," Bill said, shuffling so nervously in his seat that he nearly dropped the street guide.

"I must get myself a sat nav. system," said Pete almost to himself as he watched Bill struggle to get the street map under control again.

"This is it, Wellington Road Estate. Third turn on the

right."

"Yes, Mother," said Pete with a grin. "Will that be the one after the second?"

Bill realised how short he must have sounded and laughed himself. "Or the one before the fourth," he said. Both men began laughing, easing their tension a little.

Peter turned into Massey Street. It was obvious from the condition of the road surface and street furnishing that this area was low on the council's list for upgrading and maintenance. The few people that they saw seemed to almost limp down the street. They all looked the same, scruffy dowdy clothing, blank expressions on their faces and a hopeless haunted look of despair in their eyes.

"There it is," said Bill pointing to Armstrong Terrace.

"Jesus," gasped Pete. "What a dump."

He stopped the car at the end of the terrace and switched off the engine. He could almost feel the hopeless air of poverty percolating into the car from the street. *This was going to be no picnic*, he thought as he opened the car door and nearly stepped into a large pile of dog excrement. They took a few moments to check the immediate area before heading into Armstong Terrace. Everything looked grey. It was as if a grey damp blanket had descended and covered the street, laying heavily everywhere. Pete shuddered. "Come on, let's find number forty-seven," he said to Bill and set off down the terrace.

If the street had been grim where they stopped, compared to the terrace, it looked like a pristine boulevard. There was rubbish strewn all over. Every garden was filled with the waste that only humans could discard and the terrace path was a mine field of used needles, condoms and more dog faeces. The smell was enough to make any normal person gag and both men were tempted to hold their handkerchiefs over their mouths and noses. They walked slowly down the terrace both feeling as if they were being watched. Bill had noticed a filthy net curtain twitch as they passed one of the terrace houses. *One to remember for later,* he thought.

They stopped outside number forty-seven. There was nothing remarkable or different about this small house. It looked just like all the others, neglected and in disrepair. They approached the front door and optimistically knocked. After the third time of knocking, they decided there would be no answer. Donning a pair of thin rubber gloves, Pete grasped the door handle, turned it and pushed. The resistance he felt told him it was locked! "Let's try around the back."

Both men made their way back into the terrace and followed the central path to the far end. They came to a high brick wall, and the path branched out left and right in a 'T' Junction. They took the left path and followed it to the back of the terrace. The rear of the terrace was made up of small yards, one for each house, surrounded by a wall tall enough to prevent anyone looking over. Each house had a wooden gate, although most were either missing or hanging off by the hinges. They worked out which gate was number forty-seven's and, pushing it out of the way, entered the rear yard. They were faced with piles of rubbish and rubble that they negotiated with extreme care. A fall here could result in a broken bone or bad cut, neither to be recommended looking at the dirt covering everything. They approached a half- glazed door. The glass was cracked and so filthy that nothing could be seen through it. This time they did not bother to knock. Bill pulled on his rubber gloves, grabbed the door handle, turned and pushed. It never moved, this one was locked also.

"Right," said Pete, "stand back, I'll soon have this open."

He was just about to throw the brick he had picked up through the glass panel of the door when Bill's restraining hand grabbed his arm.

"No, boss, don't. If we break in without a warrant and there is something in there, we'll totally fuck the investigation up. Any defence lawyer would have a field day."

Pete lowered his arm. "Christ thanks, Bill, you're right I could have jeopardised everything. Let's get back to the car, I need to organise a search warrant. God knows how long that will take, but, until it happens, we'll need twenty-four-hour surveillance on the house. I want to know everyone who comes and goes into that place." Both men carefully crossed the yard again and made their way back to the car. *Patience really is a copper's virtue,* thought Pete as he opened the car door and got inside.

It took Pete about thirty minutes to organise the surveillance teams. They would work in pairs, one watching the front and one at the rear, and rotate pairs every twelve hours. A bastard of a job Pete knew, but it had to be done. Obtaining the search warrant, however, was another thing. Pete had called the superintendent to ask for permission to get the warrant. The superintendent gave authority and Pete contacted the MIR to get one of his team to contact a magistrate and obtain the warrant. There was an immediate delay as, apart from Alan Stanton, all members of the team were out of the offices on various enquiries. Alan promised he would allocate the task to the first team member who came free. Pete thanked him and informed him they were heading back to the office.

Chapter 39
Horkshire General Infirmary, NHS Toxicology Laboratory

Darren Leger swept into the laboratory, slightly flustered and clutching a large package. He had left the office hurriedly a few minutes ago after receiving a phone call on his supervisor's extension. Michael Drake, and his three colleagues in the lab, stopped what they were doing as Darren asked them to pay attention. *What's all this about?* wondered Michael, the way Darren was behaving something was seriously up.

"OK, guys, I've just come from the director's office. He had a police officer with him and this package. We are to drop everything else and do full spectrum analysis on these samples. Michael, you remember that one you did the other day?"

"What, the one that came back all clear," replied Michael, a sickly feeling beginning to form in the pit of his stomach?

"Yes. Well, it seems another seven bodies have been discovered, all found in similar circumstances. The post-mortems have uncovered no obvious cause of death so the next stage is to see if we can find anything. Right, we have four computers capable of doing these tests so let's each take a sample and see what we can find. If we get a result on the first four we'll move onto the other three." Darren opened the package and issued one sample to each technician. With trembling hands Michael took his and started the test.

After three hours the four technicians had completed the tests and printed out the results. They handed the sheets to Darren for him to collate the results. Michael watched carefully as Darren pored over the printouts. He knew what his sheet showed. Traces of a highly toxic substance had been found in the tissue sample he had tested. The computer had identified the substance as a deadly poison, CURARE!

Darren's face turned paler and paler as he worked his way through the results. Finally, reaching behind him, he pulled up a bench stool and flopped back onto it. The others gathered round, anxious to know if all the results were the same. They knew immediately they were when Darren whispered.

"Jesus Christ, what have we found here?"

He reached for the telephone and dialled the director's extension. It was answered immediately.

"The results of the first four tissue samples are in," he said. "Can I come to your office sir?"

If the technicians didn't realise the seriousness of the situation before, they did when they heard Darren use the word 'sir'. As Darren left the lab, he instructed his group to test the remaining samples. He had no doubt in his mind that the results would be the same.

Andy Bower had been sat outside the director's office for over three hours, bored to death. After he had drunk his third cup of the brown sludgy liquid that was labelled coffee, from the machine, he was feeling a little grumpy. *Christ, you waste some time hanging around in this job,* he thought. He was just about to start recounting the flowers on the 1960s wallpaper that covered the reception area walls when the door opened and Darren Leger walked in.

"I think you should see this as well," he said to Andy as he knocked on the director's door. Darren walked into the office, closely followed by Andy, after the director had called for them to come in.

"Please sit down," requested the director, a distinguished looking man called Thomas Eldon. He took the bundle of papers that Darren offered him and, after placing his half eye spectacles onto the bridge of his nose, commenced to read the reports. Andy watched anxiously as Dr Thomas Eldon slowly read through each sheet. He could see the concern creeping into Eldon's pale grey eyes and wished he would hurry up and finish so they could know the results. Thomas Eldon finally placed the last sheet on his desk, removed his spectacles, and looked steadily at Andy.

"It would seem, officer, that we have a consensus. The tests results for each of these four samples show the same thing. They all show traces of the same toxic substance. That, in itself, is serious enough but, it is what that substance is, that gives me real concern."

Swallowing down the lump in his throat, Andy asked. "What is the substance, Doctor?"

"It is a highly toxic poison called CURARE," the doctor replied.

"Isn't that what South American Indians used on their arrow heads when they were hunting?" asked Andy.

"That is one area where the substance can be used officer, but there are other ways in which this substance can be used. There is one in particular that could have a significant bearing on your investigation."

"What would that be please, sir?" Andy asked.

"Mr Leger, would you like to explain to the officer?"

"Well," started Darren Leger. "Curare is sometimes used medically. Because it has the capacity to totally immobilise a person, almost paralyses them, in fact, it is used in some types of surgery."

"You mean it is used in hospitals?" said Andy.

"Yes. In some delicate procedure involving the brain or eyes, a surgeon would administer it when they want the patient to be totally relaxed and still."

"Do all hospitals have this poison on site?" Andy asked warily.

"Most major ones," was the reply.

"And does this hospital keep it?"

There was a moment's silence as Darren looked at Eldon for guidance. Eldon nodded his head slightly and Darren continued. "Yes, it's used here."

"Where would it be kept normally," asked Andy, not really liking where these questions were leading.

"It is kept in the secure cabinet in the toxicology laboratory."

"Who has access to the cabinet?"

"The only ones that have the combination to the lock are Dr Eldon and me," replied Darren nervously.

"Who supplies the hospitals with curare?"

"It's produced by the laboratory of tropical medicines at the research centre of Kew Gardens. It comes as a thick black paste. It requires no special storage requirements and has a long shelf life."

"How does it work?" Andy could see the two men were

becoming increasingly uncomfortable with his line of questioning.

"It must be introduced through the skin or via a blood vessel. It would only give someone a mild stomach upset, if swallowed."

"Do you have any stored in the lab at present?"

"I'm not quite sure about that, it's been a while since anyone requested any. I know we had some about six or seven months ago. I'd need to check." said Darren.

"I assume you keep a record of how much you have and when it is requested and who dispensed it?"

"Of course we do! It is my responsibility to ensure it is only dispensed to an authorised person," replied Darren indignantly.

"I'll need to see this cabinet and all your records please."

Darren looked to Dr Eldon for guidance once more.

"That will be fine, officer, whenever you wish."

"Now would be a good time. Thank you for your assistance, Doctor. We'll be in touch if we require a statement from you. Now lead on Mr Leger," said Andy sternly.

When Andy and Darren Leger arrived back at the toxicology lab, the technicians were crowded around the printer comparing the results of the final three samples.

"They show the same as the first four, Darren," said one of the technicians.

"I'm not surprised," replied Darren sullenly, looking at the group. "Where's Michael?"

"Oh, he wasn't feeling too good, so he went home sick."

Andy coughed to gain Darren's attention and the laboratory supervisor responded by indicating to Andy that he should follow him into his office. Standing in one corner, Andy noticed a heavy, grey coloured, cabinet. *That must be the 'not so secure cabinet'*, he thought sarcastically. Darren approached the cabinet and, turning his back on Andy so as to obstruct what he was doing, punched in the code numbers on the keypad situated on the front of the cabinet door. He turned the handle and pulled. The cabinet door opened without a sound and Darren reached in and removed a clear, airtight, polythene container and an A5 size hard backed notebook. He carried the container over to a small table in the centre of the room. Prising off the lid he took out a small parcel wrapped in greaseproof paper. Handling the parcel very carefully he slowly unwrapped what was inside. Spreading the paper out onto the table he revealed the contents. It looked to Andy like a sticky black blob, not unlike shiny 'Play Dough'. He detected no noticeable smell, but then noticed the look of disbelief on Darren's face. "What is it?" he asked.

Darren carefully re-wrapped the substance and, picking it up carefully, carried it over to a set of digital scales perched on top of the secure cabinet. He placed the package on the scales and peered at the readout. He rushed back to the table and, snatching up the notebook, began frantically to leaf through the pages. "No, this can't be right," he moaned. "There must be a mistake!" Growing slightly more agitated Andy again asked what was wrong.

"It's the curare, there's only about half the amount here that there should be. There is no record of any being issued recently. I can't believe it! There must be a logical explanation for it," he said, repeating himself.

"You said that only you and Dr Eldon had the combination to the cabinet. Could anyone else have gotten into the cabinet?

Is it ever left unattended and open whilst a quantity is being processed?"

"Well, I suppose, if we're busy, either myself or the doctor could leave the door open, slightly, whilst we dispense the substance in the lab. Then we sometimes have to take it across to the main building and if we're busy maybe we might forget to…" His words trailed off as he realised the consequences of what he was saying. He saw the look of disgust on Andy Bower's face and swallowed deeply.

"I'll need to confiscate that notebook please, Mr Leger. One of our investigation team will visit you again so you can try to explain who would have had the opportunity to take some of this substance and when that might have been. Good day sir." Andy turned on his heels and marched, stern faced, out of the office. He did not trust himself to say any more. *What a bunch of incompetent fucking morons*, he thought angrily to himself. *Someone's head should roll for this pantomime.*

Chapter 40

On the way back to the MIR Pete's mobile rang. "Hello Peter, this is Amir."

"Hi, doc, how's things?" Pete replied.

"We've had better days. However, my team has been working extremely hard and all the post-mortems have been completed. The full reports will be with you in the morning. It has been a very difficult task, especially with the bodies that were badly decomposed. The bodies were all male, approximately the same age group, thirty-five to forty-five years old as far as we can tell. We did establish one common thing, however, all the bodies had no obvious cause of death. I am fairly sure, though, that they were all asphyxiated. The only visible signs of trauma were the bruises found on their lower arms and wrists. Also, on the bodies that still had sufficient flesh on them to see, we found large red wheals, possibly as a result of being whipped! Despite the difficulties we managed to take tissue samples from all the bodies. I hope you don't mind, but rather than disturb you, I rang the MIR and they arranged for an officer to collect the samples and take them directly to the toxicology laboratory. I would imagine the results shouldn't take too long, especially since I contacted my old friend there, Dr Thomas Eldon, and stressed how urgent the matter was."

"Amir, you're a bloody marvel. Remind me I owe you an orange juice next time we meet."

"I'll hold you to that, Peter. Good luck and we'll talk soon."

"Bye, doc," responded Pete and switched off his phone. "Come on, Bill, put your foot down."

"Any news, boss?" Bill asked, as he accelerated the car through the traffic.

"Some. I'm hoping there will be more when we get back to the office. Keep your fingers crossed."

Chapter 41

Peter and Bill arrived back at the MIR just as Andy was telling the team what he had discovered. Andy stopped what he was saying and listened as Pete asked, "Who went to the toxicology unit with the tissue samples?"

"I did, boss," replied Andy.

"How did you get on?"

"Well, they uncovered something quite bizarre. All the samples tested showed signs of a toxin."

"So they were poisoned. Did they identify what the poison was?"

"Yes," replied Andy, taking a deep breath before continuing. "The poison they found was curare!"

There was a stunned silence followed by muffled whispering as the team digested what Andy had just said.

"Isn't that something the South American Indians use to tip their arrows when hunting?" Karen asked.

"Yes. It causes total paralysis to anyone or thing once it hits the blood stream."

"Where the hell do you get that from?" Pete asked.

"Well," said Andy, "it would seem that most major hospitals keep a small amount for use in delicate surgical procedures. It's used to keep a patient totally immobilised when they are, say, doing brain surgery."

"Don't tell me," said Pete, "they keep some at the Horkshire General Infirmary."

"Yes, they do, and some is missing," replied Andy.

"I don't suppose there's any chance they might know where it's gone?" asked Peter.

"It would seem their security procedures are somewhat lax. There are only two people with the combination to the secure cabinet where it is kept. However there have been occasions when it was left open and unattended."

"Ooh fucking brilliant! How irresponsible can people be? We best get SOCO down there to see if we can get anything from the cabinet."

"I've already done that, boss," replied Andy.

"Thanks, Andy, you've done a good job. Now let's have a pow wow, see exactly where we are. Is everyone here?"

All the team were present and Pete began the update. "OK, this is what we have so far," he said, turning to face a large flip chart that was placed at the front of the office. With a marker pen he began to write;

'THINGS WE KNOW'

1. 7 bodies, all male, approximately 35 – 45years old, all buried in the same way, under the carcass of a large dog!

2. No obvious indication of 'the cause of death'

3. All bodies have signs of restraints on the lower arms and wrist areas

4. Some bodies, that still have flesh on them, have lash marks to the lower back and buttocks, as well as the groin area to the front.

5. Traces of the same poison, CURARE, was found in all the bodies.

'THINGS WE NEED TO KNOW'

1. Who are these men?
2. Where are they from? Are they all local?
3. Do they have anything in common? Like occupations, hobbies, interests.
4. What are their sexual habits?
5. Do they own computers?

Pete finished writing and turned around to face the team. "Has anyone anything else to add?" There was no reply so Pete continued. "OK. The most important task is to ID these men. Let's make sure we check their DNA, dental records, fingerprints and missing persons etc. Once that's done, I want you all to work in pairs. and start visiting the home addresses of any we have identified. Make the usual enquiries, and where possible, get the next of kin to identify the body. I want you to concentrate particularly on any computers the deceased had access to. Confiscate them and get them to the technical support boys straight away. I have a feeling the answers we're looking for are somewhere in their computers. Right, get to it!"

The meeting broke up and Pete sank into his chair with a sigh. His mobile buzzed with a message. He opened it. *You look like shit, meet me at my place at eight. I've something to relax you... K.* He smiled. *Not all bad news today*, he thought. His desk phone rang. "DI Bridle," he answered.

"Hello sir, it's David Dyson, I'm the on-duty magistrate

clerk. I have a search warrant in front of me for forty-seven Armstrong Terrace if you'd like to collect it."

"Thanks, David, I'll get someone right over. Bill, with me, Alan, get a locksmith down to forty-seven Armstrong Terrace straight away, will you? It's time to get some answers."

Chapter 42

Bill had parked the car just up the street from Armstrong Terrace. The weather was again dull and damp adding to the still depressing atmosphere that seemed to hang like a shroud over the area. "Did the locksmith say how long he might be?" Pete asked.

"He couldn't say exactly what time he'd be here. He said he was trying to get an old lady back into her flat in Blackwell Street. Apparently, she'd locked herself out and was in a real panic as she'd left a pan of stew on."

"Right," said Pete and returned to his thoughts of what they might find inside number forty-seven.

About half an hour later a white Transit van pulled up behind them. A small chubby man leaped out of the driver's door and made his way around to the rear of the vehicle. He was wearing red overalls with the logo 'Wright of Entry' written across the back, in pale blue letters. He collected a flip top toolbox from inside the van and wandered up to the police officer's car. He tapped on the window and Bill opened it. "I'm Tony Wright, locksmith," he said. "Sorry I couldn't get here sooner."

"That's OK, mate," replied Bill. "I'm Sergeant Bill Hodge

and this is Detective Inspector Peter Bridle. The house we need to get into is down that terrace over there." The officers got out of the car and, with the locksmith following, made their way to forty-seven Armstrong Terrace.

"We'll go in through the front door," said Pete, almost to himself.

"Right oh," replied Tony Wright.

"This is it," said Bill, stopping at the end of the rubbish strewn path that led down to number 47. "Over to you Mr Wright."

Tony Wright stopped at the front door and placed his toolbox on the floor beside him. He looked carefully at the door before gently turning the handle and pushing. As had happened when the police tried it, the door did not move. Wright rattled it to see if there was any movement at all. It remained firmly closed. "Looks as if it's double locked. Yale lock at the top and mortice at the bottom, provided they're not too rusty it shouldn't take me long."

He opened his toolbox and took out a bunch of skeleton keys. He began to try each one in the lock below the door handle. After a few moments he seemed satisfied that he had found a suitable one. After exerting considerable pressure and twisting it one way and then the other, he was rewarded with a satisfying clunk!

"There that's that one done, now for the other little bugger." He replaced the skeleton keys back into the toolbox and pulled out a rolled-up wallet. Untying the tape securing the roll he unrolled the wallet and placed it down on the ground. It contained several rows of metal hooks. He stood up and closely checked the Yale lock he was about to work on. Satisfied, he selected two hooks from the roll and, after inserting them into the lock, he began to jiggle them around. His concentration was something to see as he manipulated the hooks inside the lock. "Bingo!" he said and, keeping the hooks in position, he turned the handle and pushed the door open.

"Thanks, Mr Wright, if you wouldn't mind waiting in your van, please, I'll call you when we need the place securing," Bill said. Wright collected up his gear and headed off down the path. Bill turned to say something to Pete but he was already inside the house. Bill pushed his way through the narrow opening and joined Pete in the dingy hallway. The place smelt fusty but not as bad as the two men feared it might. "Where do we start?" Bill asked.

"We'll check down here first then work our way upstairs. You take the front I'll go through to the back."

On his way to the kitchen Pete passed a door in the hallway that he couldn't associate with a room. *These houses are only 'two up and two down'*, he thought, *I wonder where that leads? Well, we'll find out in a minute.* He proceeded to the back of the house and checked around the kitchen. It was as he suspected it would be, filthy and unused. "No one's cooked Sunday lunch in here for a long time," he said to himself. He tried to open the back door. It was locked, as he knew it would be. *I must remember to get Wright to check if it has been opened recently before we leave*, he thought. Finding nothing of obvious note he made his way back to the hallway. There he met Bill. "Find anything?" he asked.

"Nothing of any use to us"

"Now let's see what's behind this," Peter said indicating the other additional door in the hallway. He slowly turned the doorknob and pushed. The door did not move.

"Try pulling it," said Bill. Pete pulled the door towards

him, it opened.

"Clever bastard," he said, as he peered into the darkness. He could just make out a set of stairs disappearing down into the gloom. He groped on the wall and located a light switch. He flicked it on and proceeded down the stairs.

Chapter 43

Pete stopped at the bottom of the stairs and slowly looked around. He absorbed the scene with a professional eye. He noticed the cold, bare, concrete floor, the discarded handcuffs lying on the filthy table. The upturned chair and the rusty iron ring hanging from the crumbling brick wall directly opposite the stairs. His eyes were involuntarily drawn to the large dark stain that covered the floor below where the iron ring hung.

"What the hell had caused that?" he said to himself. He exhaled and watched, fascinated by the grey vapour cloud that drifted lazily up towards the flaking ceiling. He advanced into the cellar, conscious of where he placed his feet. Bill joined him. He also stood silently taking everything in.

"What do you think Bill?"

"I think we need SOCO down here as soon as possible. This could be a murder scene."

"I agree, let's look upstairs first though, we may find something up there as well."

The two detectives climbed out of the cellar and made their way back down the narrow hallway. They arrived at a door in the wall that opened onto the main staircase. They climbed gingerly up it. The top floor of the house was made up of a small landing, a grubby bathroom and toilet, and two bedrooms. It was the largest bedroom that interested the pair most. The smaller room, at the rear of the floor, was empty. The front bedroom was sparsely furnished. The two men entered slowly, pulling on rubber gloves as they advanced through the doorway. The room contained a single bed, pushed up tight against one wall, a small wardrobe, a dressing table with mirror, and a stool. There were fitted cupboards either side of the chimney breast. "You take the wardrobe, I'll check the cupboards."

"OK," replied Bill, making his way across the room to where the scruffy looking cabinet stood. Carefully he turned the small catch that secured the two overlapping doors and pulled. The doors opened smoothly, obvious to Bill that they had been used recently. He peered inside. Suspended from a single rail was a clothes hanger. Draped over the hanger was a shiny, black, rubber, suit. Bill thought it looked like a cross between a basque and a swimming costume, with a plunging front and low back. On the floor of the wardrobe stood a pair of thigh length black patent leather boots with four-inch stiletto heels. "Kinky," muttered Bill.

Over by the chimney Pete found that both built in cupboards were empty. He turned his attention to the dressing table. There were traces of make up on the surface and smudges on the mirror. *With a bit of luck there will be some prints on here*, he thought. There were two small drawers in the front of the dresser and Pete open the lefthand side one first. It contained a selection of cosmetics, mostly tubes of vivid red lipstick and very pale foundation cream. He carefully closed it and opened the righthand side one. It appeared, at first, to be stuffed full of dark hair clippings. Pete took a pen from his pocket and hooked a piece of hair. He pulled it from the drawer to see it form into a straggly black wig. Beneath the wig he saw a pair of long black silk gloves. He carefully replaced the wig back inside the drawer and closed it. He turned to check the bed but found that Bill was already looking at it. On top of the thin, single, mattress that lay at an angle across the bedstead, was thrown a sleeping bag. Bill carefully lifted it but found nothing beneath it. He hoped they could obtain some DNA from it. He crouched down to look under the bed, but again found nothing of interest. As he stood up, he noticed scratch marks etched into the dirt on the floorboards. These led away from the bed, roughly in line with the bed legs. The bed had been pulled out, and, judging by the depth of the scratches, more than once. He called Peter over. "What do you think, boss?"

"I think we should pull it out and see what's back there," said Pete. Taking one end each, the two police officers gently eased the bed away from the wall. Once they had the bed clear they were able to inspect the floorboards. It quickly became obvious to them that the boards closest to the wall were loose. Bill carefully worked his finger between two boards and pulled upwards. The board lifted. He removed a second to reveal a space beneath.

The space below the floorboard was about forty-five centimetres deep. Pete peered into the void and saw two items. The first he recognised as a riding crop, used by horse riders to encourage their mounts to quicken up. The second object, he was not so sure about. Without touching it he tried to see what it was. After a moment he realised he was looking at a parcel of some kind, wrapped in dark coloured greaseproof paper. He carefully removed both objects and placed them on the floor. "Well," he said to Bill. "I know what that is," pointing to the riding crop. "But as to what is wrapped inside that paper, I dread to think."

"Definitely one for the SOCO boys to open I think," said Bill. "What next Pete?"

"Leave everything as it is. It is going to need a full SOCO examination. Let's go, time marches on. We need to confirm this is the place where the murders occurred. I want to nail this evil bastard as soon as I can!"

Chapter 44

The two detectives thanked Tony Wright for his help and allowed him to leave. Bill had contacted SOCO by radio and had been given an ETA of twenty-five minutes. Whilst the pair waited in the car Pete put through a call to the MIR. He spoke to Alan Stanton. "How are things back there, Alan?"

"Moving along nicely thanks, but there are a few things you need to be aware of though."

"OK, go ahead."

"Well, the PRO has been on, it seems someone let the cat out of the bag about the other bodies and the press have got hold of it. She said she can stall them for a while, but she'll need a press release from you as soon as you can. The superintendent called for an update. I filled him in. Oh, and the good news is, the team have been working their bollocks off, and have managed to identify all the bodies. I think the super must have rattled a few cages because I've never seen things move so fast."

"Wow! That is good news. How did we identify them so quickly? Has anything been done about visiting next of kin and home addresses etc.?"

"Yes, Karen's organised the team to do it. Division have

supplied some uniform staff to take statements and arrange for the next of kin to be taken to the mortuary to formally identify the bodies. Most of the deceased were identified through DNA samples. One was cross-matched to a missing person photograph."

"That's a great job. We're waiting for SOCO at Armstrong Terrace but they shouldn't be too long, then we'll head back. I'll thank everyone when I get there. Looks like I could be redundant before long."

"OK, boss, just one more thing before you go. Karen asked if you could ring her. She's something she wants to run by you."

"Right, I'll do it now." Pete finished his conversation, got out of the car, as if to stretch his legs, and dialled Karen's mobile. Karen answered. "Can you talk or should we wait until tonight?" he asked.

"Tonight, will be fine," she replied in a light-hearted voice that indicated to Peter she was not alone.

"About eight!"

"No problem, bye."

Peter hung up just as two scenes of crime vehicles stopped behind his car. Bill got out of their car, joined Pete and the SOCO officers, and went back into number forty-seven. Pete briefed the SOCO staff on what he required and requested them to contact their supervisor to attend. He and Bill then left to return to the MIR. En route he updated Bill with events at the MIR then contacted Alan Stanton again to arrange a twenty-four-hour guard on the property and instructed him to tell everyone to go home when they had finished their present tasks and reconvene at 0800 hours the following morning.

"You can drop me back at the office and then get off home yourself, Bill. I'm going to head straight for the canteen when we get back, I'm famished." Bill nodded and sped off, tyres squealing. "Blimey you must be hungry too," laughed Pete, "just get us there in one piece eh!"

"No problem, boss," responded Bill, accelerating even quicker.

Chapter 45

Bill dropped Peter at the station, changed cars and made his way home. It had been an exhausting day. The adrenaline rush he had experienced at the house was now passing leaving him tired and hungry. He was looking forward to a quiet evening in with cool beer, and a hot meal. It would be nice to spend a little time with his partner, Quentin, a local architect. They had been an item for just over a year but Bill still could not bring himself to 'go public' with it at work. Of the team members, only Karen was aware, and she was sworn to secrecy until Bill thought the time was right. Despite the fact that the public face of the police was for total equality within its ranks, Bill knew that deep lying prejudices still existed. It had taken him long enough to be accepted as a black officer, now he wondered what sort of a reaction he would get for being gay as well. Quentin couldn't understand Bill's hesitancy; he had been openly gay and proud of it since his university days. *Perhaps I should bring Quentin to the next team 'piss up'*, Bill thought, *we'll see.* He tried to clear his mind and concentrated on avoiding having an accident in the heavy traffic.

Peter had made his way up to the third floor of the building where the MIR was situated. He had called his wife.

He was feeling guilty about telling her he was working late and not to wait up for him. "Say goodnight to the kids for me," had been his closing words. "What a total shit you are Bridle," he said irritably to himself.

"Did you say something, boss?" Alan Stanton asked. He had been the only one in the office when Pete got back. The rest of the team were either still completing enquires with the deceased's next of kin or, as he should be, were on their way home.

"Isn't it time you were off, Alan?"

"I'm just on my way. I thought you might want to see this list of names. It's the deceased we've identified." Alan placed a small wad of A4 size sheets of paper in front of Peter. Peter picked it up and glanced down the list, turning the stapled sheets over slowly. All the sheets were laid out the same, five vertical columns, each with a different heading. Peter looked at the headings:

'NAME', 'ADDRESS', 'AGE', 'SEX', 'MARITAL STATUS', 'OCCUPATION'.

Studying the list, Peter noticed some obvious similarities. The names, of course, meant nothing, but everyone on the list was the same sex, roughly the same age, thirty-five—forty-five years old, and all were single. None of the men appeared to have occupations that involved any heavy physical work. They all worked, in some capacity or other, for local agencies that had some involvement with children. They included a social worker, a clerk in a health centre, a child support worker. One worked for an adoption agency, and another was employed by a children's charity. There was even one who ran a children's home. Peter knew that these jobs were too closely linked to be just a coincidence. Had the murderer specifically targeted men who work in the areas of children's needs and welfare? Peter rubbed his sore eyes. As it had with Bill, the day was catching up with him. Peter realised that the longer this case went unsolved, the more pressure he and his team would come under. He also knew that the more time they spent on the investigation, the less chance they had of getting a result. Peter placed the papers on his desk, pulled his coat off the back of his chair and made his way out of the office. He knew there was nothing else he could do today. *It'll still be here in the morning*, he thought as he dropped the latch on the office door and headed for his car.

Chapter 46

Peter imagined this was how it must have felt to be in the womb. He was surrounded by warmth and softness, safe and sound. It was almost silent, only the distant sound of a woman's shallow breathing percolated his consciousness. His spent body seemed to float effortlessly; it was almost as if he was suspended above the bed where their passionate lovemaking had taken place. With half-closed eyes he looked around. The candles still burnt with a subdued glow. On the bedside table stood two champagne glasses, one bearing a lipstick stain that perfectly matched the lips of the women lying naked beside him. A half empty bottle of Moët & Chandon lay invitingly in the ice bucket, almost begging to be finished.

Pete's eyes followed the trail of discarded clothing that stretched from the bedroom, out of the door, and into the darkened lounge. It had been wild and hungry at first, like two animals who could not get enough of one other. Clothes were ripped off to expose naked flesh, as they dragged each other to the bedroom. The champagne had come later, a prelude to a long slow lovemaking that had resulted in Pete's present semi-conscious state. He looked at Karen, a swirl of mixed emotions running through his head. It was always the same at times like these, love for Karen being tempered by loathing for himself. He gently stroked her, running a finger from her forehead, down her nose and across her mouth. Before he could pull his hand away, she had lightly bitten his finger. "Ouch!" he cried playfully. Karen opened her eyes, smiled and pulled him towards her. She kissed him lightly and, before he could respond too passionately, she slipped out of his grasp and disappeared into the bathroom. Peter sat up and waited for her to return.

He didn't have long to wait. She appeared again wearing a dark blue silk dressing gown.

"That looks nice," he said.

"Thank you, kind sir," she replied. "It was a present from my lover. Pour me another glass please."

Peter refilled the lipstick-stained glass and passed it to Karen. He noticed she remained tantalisingly out of his reach. He watched her as she took a sip. She held the cold liquid in her mouth for a second, then rolled it around inside her mouth, enjoying the tingling sensation of bubbles on her tongue. "I could drink this stuff all the time," she said dreamily. "Aren't you joining me?"

"Best not. I have to drive home," Peter replied sadly.

An uncomfortable silence developed between them after Pete mentioned home. Karen spoke first. "I've been wondering. Do you think we might be able to get away together for a couple of days sometime?" Pete thought that it was highly unlikely but he did not want to disappoint Karen too much.

"Perhaps when this damned enquiry is wrapped up we may be able to arrange something."

"Right," said Karen quietly. "Oh, and talking of the job, there's something that's been bothering me and I wondered if I could run it past you." Grateful for the change of subject Peter told her to continue. "Well. Going by what you said earlier it looks like all the men were killed in the same way, using curare."

"Yes, that's correct."

"Then how did Clive Wilkinson die? His toxicology results came back negative."

"That's right," replied Peter thoughtfully. Karen always seemed to have the knack of finding something most other members of the team had missed.

"Do you think it would be worth checking it again?"

"It wouldn't do any harm. I'll get Andy on it first thing tomorrow."

The silence between them returned and Pete left the bed and went to freshen up. On his return he found that Karen had moved back into the lounge. He dressed quickly and joined her. She was sat on the sofa, gazing at the wall, the empty champagne glass still in her hand. He went over and sat beside her. He took the glass from her and placed it on the coffee table in front of them. He pulled her gently into his arms where she snuggled contentedly. "I know how much you hate it being like this," he said, "but you know the situation."

"It's OK," she replied softly. "I understand and if this is the only way it can be then I'm happy with it."

He kissed her lovingly and left.

Chapter 47

It was nine o'clock and the team had been at the MIR for an hour. During that period Pete had listened intently as each member had given an update on their previous day's tasks. All the bodies had now been officially identified. The list of the deceased, that Pete had been given the evening before, was now displayed on the MIR wall chart. Pete began his summing up after everyone had helped themselves to a hot drink and the almost compulsory canteen bacon sandwich!

"As you can see things are beginning to fall into place. Hopefully there are no more bodies lying about out there. It is now emerging that we are probably dealing with a single killer. Apart from one body, we now know all the deceased were killed in the same way. There are also other similarities with these men." Pete turned and pointed to the wall chart. "If you look at the list you can see that these males all fall into nearly identical categories. Their ages, occupations, marital status, are all very similar. They all worked in areas that deal with child welfare. We need to find a motive for the killings and quickly.

"Bill, get a couple of the team to see the technical support unit. We need to know what was on these men's computers and if there's anything with a common theme to it. Andy, check with the toxicology lab, see if they still have the original tissue sample from Clive Wilkinson, if they have, ask them to re-test it. If they haven't, get over to the mortuary and see if you can obtain another one. The body hasn't been released for burial yet so you should be OK. Either way, make sure it's tested thoroughly, stand over them if you have to. Karen, Mike, go down to Armstrong Terrace. I need an update on what SOCO has found there. Alan, hold the fort here please. I need to go and brief the boss then pop to see the PRO. No doubt the press will have been nattering for an update. OK team let's go, time and tide etc."

The team dispersed and Peter sat down at his desk to gather his thoughts. After a few minutes thinking he left, heading first to see the superintendent and then on to see Maggie Hebden at the press office.

Chapter 48

After briefing the superintendent and going over the latest press release with the PRO, Peter returned to the MIR. As he entered the office Bill beckoned him over. He indicated for Pete to sit down and slowly open the manila-coloured folder that was sitting on his desk. Peter pointed at the folder and asked. "Results from the tech support guys?"

"Yes, and it makes very interesting reading. It would seem all the dead males are 'naughty little boys who enjoy being punished.' All the computers we confiscated show that they all visit S&M sites on a regular basis."

"OK. So that's another thing they all have in common."

"Ah yes, but there's more. George Blake managed to get into their email systems and it would seem that they all had contact with a Dominant from the same site. They all met a woman called Melinda!"

"Can we trace her through the site?"

"George reckons not. He says these types of sites are so secure you can never hack into them. They're set up in such a way as to be totally safe for the punters and the Dominants as well."

"Fuck," hissed Pete in frustration. "Is there anything else

there that might be of use to us?"

"There is just one thing."

"What's that?"

"All the men arranged to meet the woman at the same place. FORTY-SEVEN ARMSTRONG TERRACE!"

"Bingo!" Pete shouted. "Let's hope SOCO turn something up there."

Pete could feel a satisfactory tingle run through his body. He was confident they were really onto something now. *We just need a couple more pieces to fall into place and we might start to see what the jigsaw looks like*, he thought. With that his desk phone rang. He snatched it up and answered. "Hello. DI Bridle speaking."

"Hello, boss, it's Andy. I'm at the lab and something has turned up."

"What have you got, Andy?"

"Well, we did as you asked and contacted the lab. I spoke to the supervisor there, Darren Leger. He confirmed to me that the original tissue sample from Wilkinson would have been incinerated after the results were completed. On hearing that, I arranged to collect a new sample from the mortuary and then brought it here to be tested. I did as you told me and stood over them whilst it was tested again. I made sure Leger carried out the test. Guess what? It tested positive for a poison. He identified it as curare, looks like we've got a full house!"

"Andy, did you find out who did the original test?"

"Yes, it was a technician named Michael Drake."

"Have you spoken to him?"

"No, he's off sick at the moment, so I couldn't. Leger told me that he never thought to question the results because Drake had so much experience in the field, and he trusted his work.

He went on to mention that Drake was the senior technician, and as such, he sometimes covered for Leger when he is away."

"Did Drake have access to the secure cabinet when he was covering for Leger?"

"Hang on, I'll ask him." There was a short silence before Andy spoke again. "Yes, he has full access to all the secure cabinets in the lab when he is in charge."

"Good work, Andy. Leave someone there to take a statement. You get Drake's home address and come back here. I think a little home visit to see Mr Drake might be called for."

Peter's head was spinning with unanswered questions. *Another piece had just fallen into place. Had Drake stolen some of the poison from the secure cabinet and falsified the records to cover it up? Where was Drake now? And of course, the $64,000 question, what had he done with the curare?*

Chapter 49

It was later that afternoon before all the members of the MIT finally returned to the office. Peter decided to hold a quick debrief just to see where they stood. Bill went first. He quickly informed the team of the results the tech boys had retrieved from the deceased men's computers. He explained how they showed that all the males had visited the same Dominant, a female called 'Melinda', and that these meetings all took place at forty-seven Armstrong Terrace. "Do we know who owns the property," asked Peter. "Yes, it belongs to a scrote, named Sean Lawson. He has previous for minor offences of supplying Class A stuff. We spoke to him and he said that the property is rented out to a woman who pays him in cash at a pre- arranged meeting place. He has no details of her and says he cannot describe her as it's always dark when he meets her. He's a really helpful little shit boss."

"OK, thanks, Bill, if we need to we can get the drug squad to lean on him a bit, see if that improves his memory."

Karen went next. She explained what SOCO had found at Armstrong Terrace. "Considering the size of the place," she said, "SOCO have concluded that it is, crime wise, very clean. They've found only one partial fingerprint on the handle of the riding crop that was hidden under the floorboards. They've taken samples from the wig, and scrapings from the cellar floor. These will be checked for DNA, as will the mattress and sleeping bag. The package of dark sticky substance, found under the floorboards, has been sent away for analysis. The crop has also gone with it as there is evidence that the crop had been dipped in the substance. Hopefully the results will be back first thing tomorrow."

"Where is the package and crop being sent for testing?" Peter asked.

"To the toxicology laboratory at the hospital," replied Karen, a puzzled look crossing her face.

"Andy. You best go there first thing and oversee those tests. We don't want any more cock ups from them. Right, you can fill everybody in with what you found out there today."

Andy gave his report to the rest of the team. Karen then realised why Peter had asked where the crop and package was being sent for testing.

"Bill, Karen, I want you to concentrate on this character Michael Drake, the technician from the lab. I need everything you can find on him. His background, bank accounts, hobbies, interests etc. See what you can come up with. Andy has his home address but I don't want him visited until I have some idea what we might be dealing with. The rest of you, I want everything double checked. Make sure all statements have been taken. Ensure the next of kin are informed about the delays on the bodies being released for burial etc. No loose ends please people. We need everything as tight as a frog's arse, and we know how tight they are, don't we? OK let's get to it!"

Peter now knew that patience was the most vital element of their enquiry. Everything was coming together nicely but he knew that one mistake could blow the whole thing out of the water.

Chapter 50

The following morning those members of the team that had tasks to perform away from the MIR had already gone by the time Peter arrived. It had taken him longer than usual to attend to Jenny and the kids, she was definitely getting worse. The thought filled him with fear and sadness. Bill thrust a cup of hot strong tea into his hand and invited him to sit down at the desk occupied by Karen. He took a mouthful of the tea before removing his coat and settling in next to Karen. Karen looked into his eyes, and saw the hurt there, she knew something was on his mind and she prayed silently that it would not affect her.

"We've done some background work on Mr Drake and it's thrown up some very interesting things." Peter leant back in his chair and told Bill to continue.

"Michael Drake was born on the fourteenth of February 1977. His mother died in giving birth and there is no record of the father. He was in the care of the local authority all his life until he was seventeen. He lived in various children's homes, the last one being the Weybrooke Children's Care Home."

Peter immediately looked up at Bill, concern written across his face. "Did you say Weybrooke?"

"Yes. Why does it mean something to you?"

Pete looked across the office. "Tell them, Alan."

Alan Stanton, the office manager and ex-detective, left his desk and joined the group. He had been listening to the conversation and his ears pricked up when he heard Weybrooke mentioned.

"In early 1999 we had an anonymous report that children were being abused at that home. The allegations involved the couple who managed the home at the time, a man called Henry Poole and his wife Barbara. Despite a very detailed investigation we found nothing. The children living there were too frightened to say anything. We managed to locate a few of the old residents who had left the area but no one was prepared to talk to us. The case was left on file but the story caused such a ruckus that the local authority decided to close the place down."

"Any idea what happened to Mr and Mrs Poole?" Bill asked Alan.

"Rumour had it that they disappeared from the area. I did hear they might have gone to Spain but we had no reason to follow up on that as none of the children were prepared to make a complaint."

"Do we have a list of all the residents at the time when Drake was there?"

Karen passed Peter a piece of paper with a list of fifteen names printed on it. Bill and Karen waited patiently whilst Peter read the names on the list. Peter was about halfway down when a name seemed to jump out at him. He looked at it again and again. Melinda Brown! *This is too much of a coincidence,* he thought, his heart beating faster. He lifted his eyes slowly and stared at Karen and Bill.

"Have you seen this name?"

"Yes," they replied in unison.

"Hell, we need to do some digging on her. See if we can find her. We need to know if she is still in contact with Drake. Bill, get onto it, make it a priority. Karen, you come with me."

"Where are we going?"

"We're off to see the mysterious Michael Drake.

Peter drove in silence, Karen glancing anxiously sideways at his troubled face.

Karen slipped her hand onto Pete's thigh and rubbed it gently. He glanced across at her and smiled weakly. "Are you all right?" she asked.

"Yes," he replied, then said, "well no, I'm not really."

"Is it Jenny?"

"Yes, oh, Karen she's getting worse and there's nothing I can do. I feel so bloody helpless."

"Pull over," she said. Pete pulled the car off the road, stopped, then turned to face Karen. She drew him to her and held him close, feeling his silent sobs pounding her chest. She tenderly stroked his head and waited for his sorrow to pass. After a few moments he raised his head, kissed her lightly on the lips, and said "Thanks. I don't know what I'd do without you."

"Come on," she said. "We've got a murder to solve."

Chapter 51

Michael sat slumped in an armchair, a half empty bottle of Chivas Regal malt whiskey stuffed between his legs. The curtains were drawn allowing only a shadowy light to percolate into the room. He listened to the shrill shrieking voice that seemed to come at him from everywhere within the darkened room.

"You stupid cunt. You've panicked again and most likely this time you've led them here. I don't know why I stay with you. You can't do anything right."

"I'm sorry," mumbled Michael, "I just got scared. When I found out they had more tissue samples to test, I knew they'd discover curare in them. It stood to reason they would then re-test another sample, and eventually want to speak to me about it."

"You could have bluffed it out. You know yourself those tests can be inconclusive. Well, if they turn up here, you'll have to deal with it then, you know I can't handle anything like that."

Michael reached down for the bottle and, raising it to his mouth, took a large swig.

"And that won't help either. Pull yourself together or we'll really end up in the shit."

"Shut up! Shut up!" Michael shouted. "I can't stand it any more. You're driving me fucking mad." Michael heard the callous laughter as he collapsed onto the floor, the pain in his head rendering him unconscious. He lay prostrate on the threadbare carpet, the voice now silent.

When he woke up it was totally dark. He lay motionless, his mouth filled with the bitter taste of bile which always accompanied the attacks. Listening for anything that might tell him, she was still there, he slowly staggered to his feet and made his way carefully to the bathroom. The nausea hit him again as he reached the wash basin and he vomited into the grubby white bowl. He gingerly raised his head and looked at the ashen face that stared back vacantly at him. *She was right*, he thought, *booze never was the answer.* He rinsed his mouth, opened the cabinet door and rummaged about to find some pain killers. Finding a dog-eared strip of Paracetamol, he tore off two and swallowed them dry. He walked into the kitchen, switched the kettle on, and proceeded to make a cup of instant coffee. The milk he found in the refrigerator was off and he nearly threw up again after sniffing the sour-smelling liquid. He decided black would be fine. Clutching the mug with trembling hands he carried the coffee into the lounge and slumped exhausted back into the chair. He took a slurp of the coffee, it felt like trying to swallow cardboard, he gagged but persevered. He forced down a second mouthful. This time his stomach didn't try to reject it and soon the caffeine kicked in and he began to feel a little more human.

He sat quietly turning over in his mind what had happened. She was right. They had nothing on him. When challenged about the test he would tell them he followed all the procedures correctly and that was what the result was. That arsehole Leger would confirm that any tests can sometimes prove to be inconclusive. *Yes*, he thought, *that's what I'll do. The bastards won't get me*. At that moment the doorbell rang!

Chapter 52

Michael opened the door. A police warrant card was thrust into his face. He stepped back to see who was holding the card. There were two people standing in the hallway, a well-built male and a petite female. "Michael Drake?" the male asked. "We're police officers, do you mind if we come in for a little chat?" Before Michael had a chance to reply they had pushed past him into the lounge. He could see by the disgusted looks on their faces that the smell of stale vomit and alcohol still hung heavily in the air.

"I understand you've not been feeling too well, Mr Drake, hope it's nothing serious," said the female. "Please sit down you don't look too good."

"Thank you," replied Michael, relieved to sit down. "I've had a stomach bug but I'm beginning to feel a little better."

"I'm Detective Inspector Bridle and this is DC Karen James. We're from the Horkshire Police Major Incident Team. I understand you work at the toxicology lab at the hospital, is that correct?"

Michael was somewhat taken aback by the brusqueness of the question. He took a moment to collect his thoughts. He was conscious of the female officer moving around the room behind him. "Yes, that is correct, I have worked there for about eight years or so. Why is there a problem?" Michael tried to remain calm and keep his voice strong and confident. He tried to hide his hands under his thighs to prevent the officers seeing how much they were trembling.

"I understand you conducted a toxicology test on a tissue sample a few days ago Mr Drake. What was the result of that test sir?"

"I'm not quite sure what you are referring to Inspector. We carry out hundreds of tests in the lab on a daily basis."

"Come, come, Mr Drake, surely you must remember this one, the sample came from the mortuary as an urgent request. It came from the body of a murder victim. You don't mean to tell me you get that type of thing in everyday, do you?"

Michael tried to relax, he began to feel queasy again and he tried desperately to swallow. "Oh, I think I remember the one you mean. Yes, I did a full spectrum analysis. I seem to recall it came back as negative. It's all in the report I gave to my supervisor."

"How do you account for the fact, that we have had a second sample tested and this proved positive for a poisonous substance? That poison has been identified as curare. Do you know what curare is, Mr Drake?"

Michael took a deep breath and replied. "I cannot explain that, but it is not unusual in these types of tests to get fluctuations in results. I'm sure my boss would concur with that, oh and yes, I do know what curare is. As a matter of fact, we keep a small amount at the lab."

"Do you have access to it?"

"Sometimes, when I am covering for Darren Leger, I have the authority to dispense the substance."

"Do you know Melinda Brown?" The question came sharply and unexpectedly from the female standing behind him. Surprised that she should ask that question, Michael turned slowly to look at the woman. His mind was spinning. *Where had she got that from?* he asked himself. *How much do they know? Are they bluffing?* He decided to answer honestly and try to establish what they really knew about Melinda.

"Yes. I once knew someone by that name. We grew up together in an orphanage. She was a couple of years older than me so left before I did."

"Did you keep in contact with her?"

"No, I'm afraid not."

"So you've no idea where she might be now?"

"No."

"Do you know anyone who might be aware of her whereabouts?"

"No."

"Do you own a computer, Mr Drake?"

"No."

"Do you have access to one?"

Again, Michael answered no, in a bored voice. "Look, Inspector, are you going to tell me what all this is about?"

"No," replied Peter sarcastically.

"Mind if we have a look around the flat?" Karen asked as she moved towards where she imagined the bedroom would be.

"Would it make any difference if I said no?"

"Not really. Unless you've got something to hide and if you have then we'd just get a search warrant. You don't have anything to hide do you Mr Drake?"

Michael remained tight lipped and watched as the officers

173

left the room to have a look round. "Huh," he said quietly to himself. "Look all you like, you bastards won't find a thing." Despite his bravado Michael felt the nausea returning and dashed to the bathroom. When he returned, ashen faced and shaking, they were waiting for him. Peter Bridle approached him and stood almost nose to nose with him.

"We may need to talk to you again," he said threateningly. "Not thinking of leaving town, are you?"

"No."

"Good. Thank you for your time, Mr Drake." Peter turned and followed Karen towards the door. "Oh, just one thing, you don't happen to have a photograph of Melinda Brown do you?"

"Sorry no I haven't. As I said before I lost contact with her years ago."

"OK. Hope you're feeling better. Goodbye, Mr Drake, don't bother seeing us out, we'll find our own way." Peter closed the front door behind him and hurriedly caught up with Karen. "That man is hiding something. I'm sure he knows where Melinda Brown is. Let's put a tail on him."

"OK, Pete, I'll get straight onto it when we get back to the office."

Back in the flat Michael decided that he must find another hiding place for his computer. It would soon be found behind the kitchen shelves if the police conducted a more thorough search.

Chapter 53

Things were slowly grinding to a halt as they seemed to do at some stage in all major enquiries. Peter was becoming more and more frustrated with their lack of progress. He was also getting pressure from above to resolve the case. The round the clock surveillance on Michael Drake had proved fruitless. He had been under observation for over a week and had done nothing suspicious. He had returned to work, attended the gymnasium, gone to a pub one evening with some work colleagues, but other than that, he had gone nowhere. The only new thing the team discovered about Drake was his previous involvement with a woman. They found out that he had been in a long relationship with a woman called Adele Tomlinson. The details were very scant but they had been together for about eight years. It appeared to have fizzled out about the time Drake started to work at the laboratory. Pete instructed the two team members who had found out about the woman to continue with their enquiries and locate her if possible.

During a quiet period in the office, Pete noticed a small group from the team huddled around Bill Hodge's desk. He sauntered over to find out what they were up to. He approached the group, who, when they saw him coming, broke up. "Something going on I should know about?"

"Just an idea a few of us have been kicking about boss," replied Bill.

"Well, let's hear it then."

"OK. As you know we seem to be at a dead end. Drake is taking us nowhere and we can't find Melinda Brown or this other woman Tomlinson. We thought that, rather than we look for them, especially Brown, why don't we try to get them to come to us? There's no reason to believe that this Melinda would not take the bait."

"And how do you propose to do that?"

"We respond to Melinda over the internet and set up a meeting. Once it's arranged, we can set the trap and catch her in the act, so to speak."

Peter stood, silently playing over in his mind what Bill had said. He agreed they were going nowhere with the case, but he felt it was too dangerous to play cat and mouse with a seven-time murderer. "Sorry. We can't do it."

"Why not?" asked Bill.

"For three reasons. One it could be construed as 'entrapment', two it could be dangerous, and three we can't take the risk that we may be traced via our email address."

By now the other members of the team had gathered round and were listening intently to what was being said. "Who would it be dangerous for?" asked Karen. "We would be controlling it. We could make sure we had plenty of people at the premises and we could bug the rooms before the event. We could also ask the tech boys to set us up with a false identity linked to a children's agency or something."

"That still doesn't get around the 'entrapment' issue," replied Peter.

"We could run it past one of the lawyers at the CPS," said Alan Stanton, from his desk across the room.

"Come on, boss, let's give it a try. What have we got to lose?" said Bill.

"Yes. Let's have a go boss," echoed the rest of the team.

"OK, OK. I'll speak to the CPS, but if they say no then it's dead in the water."

Pete wondered what the best way would be to approach the CPS. He knew they were sticklers for procedures and would only agree if the operation was done strictly within the letter of the law. He felt it needed someone with a bit more 'clout' to speak to the CPS. He decided to contact Superintendent Fowler for help. He telephoned the superintendent's secretary and asked if he could see the super urgently. He replaced his phone and waited for her to ring him back. Within ten minutes he was on his way up the stairs to Fowler's office.

Peter briefed the superintendent and returned to the MIR. Fowler had listened intently to Peter's suggestion and promised to do his best to get the CPS to agree to the plan. He told Peter he would get on with it immediately and would contact him when he had some news. Pete was on his third caffeine boost when his telephone rang. The office was silent. All the team were staring intently at Pete. He seemed to be listening for ages before he said. "Thanks for the help, sir. I appreciate it. Yes, I will. Bye." Peter looked sullenly down at his desk.

"Well. What did he say, boss?"

"He said, the CPS stated that it was a very unusual and dangerous request. They thought very long and hard before agreeing to let us set it up."

"Yes!" came the cry from the room, as the team celebrated the news.

"Hold on please. The superintendent said that if we do manage to set this up then every step has to recorded and checked. Strict police procedures must be followed. He insists we do nothing that allows a defence council to punch holes in our case, there's too much hanging on it. Is that understood by everyone here?" Everyone nodded their heads in agreement. "All right, let's start planning."

Chapter 54

Peter allocated specific tasks to the team. Bill was put in charge of security. His job was to ensure that the premises at Armstrong Terrace were covered covertly during the operation by members of the team. Karen was to liaise with the Technical Support Unit (TSU). They needed audio visual surveillance equipment installing in the house, sufficient to cover all main rooms, the cellar and the two entrances. Peter called George Blake. He spoke to him at great length, making sure George knew exactly what he needed. George confirmed what was required and promised to contact Peter when it was done. Peter settled down at his desk to try to catch up on some of the paperwork that had accumulated. Alan Stanton kept most of the administrative stuff up to date but certain things like overtime and expenses needed Peter's signature. He was aware that setting up an operation like this would take time. All the team were fully occupied so Peter decided to pull rank and have an early day. He felt he needed to spend some time at home with Jenny and the kids. It also meant he might be able to catch up on some overdue sleep. He signed the final expenses claim and handed the stack back to Alan. "Right, I'm done for the day," he said. "I'll be at home, only contact me if it's urgent. Everything else can wait until the morning briefing at 0900 hours. Has anybody got any questions?" No one responded so Peter bid them all goodbye and left the office.

He drove home steadily, enjoying the drive in the late afternoon sunshine. The traffic was light and he felt himself beginning to relax. By the time he had arrived home and parked the car in the garage the sun was setting, casting long shadows across his badly kept lawn. He stood for a moment to look at the yellowing grass. *I must try to spend more time at home, this place is looking decidedly 'tatty'*, he thought. He knew, however, that it was highly unlikely he would be able to do that until this case was solved. Locking the garage door, he strolled up the path and entered the house.

Hanging his jacket on the hall stand he called out. "Hi, is anybody here? I'm home." Before he had time to ask again, he was enveloped by his two excited children.

"Daddy, Daddy, you're home. Will you play in the garden with us?"

"Of course I will. You go and get ready and I'll be out in a minute. Where's your mum?"

"She's in the kitchen getting dinner ready," replied Molly, the eldest.

"Can we play football, Dad?" James, his six-year-old son, asked.

"No, we're going to play rounders, aren't we Daddy?"

"Now you two, I don't want any arguing. There'll be plenty of time to play both. Off you go whilst I talk to your mother." The two children ran off excitedly. *Doesn't take much to bring a smile to their faces*, he thought.

He stood quietly, leaning against the door frame of the kitchen door. He watched his wife as she struggled to peel a bowl of potatoes. Her hands trembled so badly she could hardly hold the knife. He felt his heart beating against his chest wall and swallowed as the lump rose in his throat. *Life's just not bloody fair. Where is my beautiful Jenny?* He closed his eyes and imagined her dancing. She would glide around the floor as light as a feather, her wonderful pale green eyes sparkling with life. He remembered how patient she had been with him when he trod on her feet as he tried to keep up with her. She had loved to dance. Sadly, now sometimes she could only just manage to walk unaided. "Here let me do those for you," he said as he crossed the kitchen to her.

"Would you mind? I think the knife's a bit blunt," she said. "It's lovely to see you home early. The kids sound thrilled." She leant back into him as his arms encircled her and he nuzzled her neck. With difficulty she turned her head and accepted the light kiss he brushed across her lips.

"Why don't you sit down and I'll fix us a drink."

"Thanks, I will. There's a bottle of Sancerre in the fridge, it should be cool now." Reaching for her walking stick, Jenny hobbled across the floor and hitched herself up on a tall breakfast chair.

"Wouldn't you be more comfortable in the lounge?"

"Probably, but then I'd miss the pleasure of looking at you whilst you do the vegetables," she said with a smile.

"You're a hard task master," he replied and poured two glasses of the cool white wine. The children seemed to know that their parents needed a little time together. Peter had finished preparing the vegetables and chatted to Jenny about the kids and the house before they came bursting into the kitchen demanding he join them in the garden.

"Go on," said Jenny. "I can manage now."

With the children pulling his arms, Peter was dragged out into the garden to play football and rounders before the daylight disappeared.

Peter couldn't remember the last time they had all sat down as a family for a meal together. He had forgotten how the children chattered, despite their mother telling them that it was rude to speak with food in their mouths. He had also forgotten what a wonderful cook Jenny was. His mind drifted back to the time when he was only on a constable's wage. Jenny always managed to put wonderful meals on the table. It was amazing what she could do with cheap cuts of pork and beef. Wonderful casseroles and stews in winter, and salads and hams in the summer. Under Jenny's green fingers their small garden produced wonderful vegetables and flowers. Now all that was ended, Jenny struggled more and more as the weeks passed. Some days it was all she could do to get out of bed. Peter knew that, despite her objections, he was going to have to get someone in to help her. He was not looking forward to broaching that particular subject with her!

He put the children to bed. Taking the time to read both of them a story. James liked tales about pirates and spacemen, Molly listened intently to Peter as he relayed a story of a young girl and her first pony. "Do you think I could have a pony when I'm old enough?"

"We'll see sweetheart. Now, off you go to sleep."

Peter kissed his daughter goodnight, switched out the light, and rejoined his wife downstairs. They finished the bottle of wine and went to bed, falling asleep in each other's arms. That had not happened for a long time.

Chapter 55

Once again, the team was assembled at the MIR. Peter called the briefing to order then asked, if anyone had completed their task yet. Karen raised her hand. "Yes, Karen, go ahead."

"We worked all night at the Armstrong Terrace address and the place is now fully covered. We have audio and visual surveillance equipment throughout the building. The TSU boys did a great job."

"Great. Do you mind if I ask you a question?" Before Karen could answer Peter continued. "Why, if you worked all night are you here this morning and not at home, tucked up in bed?"

"I thought there might be something important at this briefing and I didn't want to miss it," replied Karen, rather embarrassed.

"Karen, I need you fresh and alert. Now go and get some rest. George will fill me in with the surveillance details. We'll see you later today." Karen collected her coat and bag as she left the office for home. She had to admit she was tired. It had been a few years since she had had to work a night shift and it didn't go down very well.

"Bill, how are we doing with the security for the

operation?"

"OK. I have organised the observers in pairs. My only concern is where best to place them in relation to the house. I don't think it will be too much of a problem but I need to go down there again and check it out. I'll have to be careful whilst I do though, walls have eyes down there. I was thinking of doing a drive-by this morning then going back after dark to finalise it."

"Right, I'll leave it with you. Take Andy with you if you want."

"Will do, boss. Andy, you're with me, let's go," said Bill.

As the two detectives were leaving, George Blake from the TSU came into the office. He approached Peter directly and said, "I've done as you asked. I'll show you it now if you've got the time."

"Blimey, George! Have you been up all night with Karen and her crew?"

"Me? Don't be daft. Night work's for owls. I'm a day bird. I knocked this up for you this morning. It looks complicated but to a genius like me it was child's play."

"Some child's play I'll bet," said Peter as he gestured for George to sit at the computer on his desk.

George quickly fired up the computer and brought up the Internet. He accessed the email section and listed the contact names. He selected a name, John Herbert. "This is the identity I have created for you. As you requested, I have made it so it appears he works for a children's charity. It has the normal service provider's security. If anybody receives an 'email' from this fictitious person they will be able to reply. The internet provider is a dummy one we created for these types of operations but if the recipient is clever enough, they'll be able to hack in and get the details of Mr Herbert. All you have to do is go onto the S&M website where the mysterious Melinda is located, get her email address and send her a message. It's that simple."

"Thanks, George, I owe you a pint for this one."

"It's my pleasure. Call me if you need anything else. Bye, Pete."

"Bye, George, see you later."

Peter sat in the chair George had vacated and began searching for the site that would lead to Melinda. "Right, you bitch, let's see if we can flush you out into the open."

Peter knew that contacting Melinda, and getting her to walk into his trap, was critical to solving the case. He didn't know how long it would be before she took the bait or indeed if she would take it. Either way, patience was the key.

Chapter 56

"Are you mad? What do you think you're doing? You know the police have been sniffing around. What if they're monitoring the computer?"

"Relax, you spineless bastard. How can they possibly trace what I'm doing? You know as well as I do the police are still in the dark ages as far as technology goes. Anyway, we can't let an opportunity like this slip through our hands. This one, sounds perfect. 'J', or John Herbert as he is really known, is a pathetic, snivelling wimp who wants mummy to punish him. I'll punish him all right."

"You're not going to invite him to the house, are you?"

"Of course I am, fool."

"But Melinda that's crazy. I have a bad feeling about this. Don't do it please."

"Shut up your whining, anyway, it's too late to worry, it's already arranged. He's coming tomorrow night at 7.30."

"God, I don't believe it. You are mad. Well, if you must do it, at least let me check the place out before you go."

"Do what you like. It makes no difference to me I'm still going through with it. You do remember why we're doing this don't you?"

"Yes," he replied in a meek voice.

"Good, now piss off out of here I'm tired."

Michael could feel one of his headaches coming on so he went to the bathroom, took two pain killers and went to bed. He dreamt, badly as always, the same dream, the dark cellar, the whip, the horror. He woke just before dawn, his vest and underpants soaked in sweat, his stomach churning.

"Don't worry," said a soothing voice. "It will be all right, I promise." He drifted off again, this time into a dreamless sleep.

Chapter 57

The following morning Peter arrived at the office early. He realised his hands were trembling slightly as he turned on his computer. "Please be there," he said to himself. The screen glowed brightly with the multi-coloured home page of the internet. Peter selected the 'email' contacts for John Herbert. He held his breath whilst the system loaded. There it was, a message from Melinda. Peter opened it and began to read.

Well, you naughty boy. So you want Mummy to punish you? Well, I can help you with that. Come alone to forty-seven Armstrong Terrace at seven thirty tonight. Enter through the front and follow the instructions pinned to the door in the hallway. Don't be late or you'll be punished even more, or is that what you want?
Ha Ha!
Melinda.
PS. Remember the code word 'AMBER'

"Yes," cried Peter. "Now we'll see who you are. Bloody hell where is everybody?"

Peter had forgotten he was early. The rest of the team

weren't due for another hour. Peter suddenly realised how hungry he was. He had slept very little and only managed a cup of tea before he left. He headed for the canteen. *Best get some food inside me*, he thought. *God knows how long this day will be.*

He passed the time over breakfast chatting with the custody sergeants from the charge room down below the MIR. The cooked breakfast was just as he liked it, large, hot and greasy. He always said if you're going to clog your arteries up, you may as well have some enjoyment whilst you're doing it. Feeling better he said goodbye to the sergeants and returned to the MIR. When he arrived, the team were waiting.

"Good morning, everybody," he said. "What a lovely day." The team looked at him suspiciously. It was not like the boss to be so cheerful first thing. "We've had a break." The team immediately sat up and paid attention, waiting to hear what had happened.

"The lovely Melinda has replied. She wants to meet us tonight at 1930. You all know what needs doing so let's get to it. No cock ups people. We're getting close to catching this murdering bitch. Now, let's get started."

There was an excited buzz going round the room as the team started to respond to Peters orders. They all knew how important this day could be. Like the boss said: NO COCK UPS!

Chapter 58

The trap was set. Peter made sure everyone was in position early. The locksmith had attended and opened the property. Nosey neighbours were instructed to ignore any suspicious coming and going. They were told it was a drugs operation. The decent ones understood. The shady ones disappeared before Peter's team arrived. Peter decided he would oversee the operation from the MIR. He felt his presence would not be required at the scene. Bill was experienced enough to handle the situation.

At Armstrong Terrace, Bill and the rest of the team had taken up their positions just as dark was falling. Observation teams were spread out along all the approaches to the address. There was no one inside. The trap would be sprung when Melinda arrived and entered the property. Bill, Karen and two burly DCs were parked up in a plain police car just out of site of the address. They would be the arrest team when the suspect arrived. Everyone was tense, a mixture of anxiety and excitement. Bill prayed nothing would go wrong. They had spent too long on this case to let her slip through the net now. He went over the plan again in his mind. He could see no flaws in it. He did a final radio check with all the team then settled down to wait. It was 1830 now, an hour to go.

Chapter 59

"Let me go first," Michael said. "I can make sure everything's clear and there are no police about. You know I've got this feeling something's going to go wrong."

"If you must, but I think you're worrying about nothing, as usual."

"I'll let you know if it's not safe."

Michael left the flat and walked to the nearest bus stop. He had decided to leave the car at home and travel by public transport. He had dressed in dark clothing to make him less conspicuous as he walked down the ill-lit alleys that surrounded the approach to Armstrong Terrace. He didn't have long to wait for a bus. He paid the fare to the main station and changed buses there for Armstrong Terrace. He got off the bus a few stops earlier than was necessary. He wanted to do as large a sweep as possible of the area on his way in towards the house.

It took him about twenty-five minutes get close to the address and during that time he had seen nothing suspicious. He checked his watch, it was 6.25 p.m. His nerves were shot due to the tension that had built up on his approach. He could do with a drink to calm himself down. He noticed the welcoming lights of the Duck and Drake public house beckoning to him. He crossed over the road and made his way to the pub, his eyes twitching from left to right searching for anything unusual. He entered the bar of the pub and walked up to the barmaid.

"Evening, love," she said, giving Michael a welcoming smile. She must have been about fifty, Michael thought, but she dressed like a teenager. She wore tight blue denim jeans, a short, close-fitting, white tee shirt with a plunging neckline that showed off her ample cleavage. Michael noticed a roll of fat bulging out from between the bottom of her shirt and the top of her jeans. He averted his eyes in disgust and asked for a large whisky. She turned and offered a small glass up to the optic containing Bells whisky. She forced two shots into the glass and placed it on the bar in front of Michael. "That will be £2.80," she said. Michael fished in his wallet and pulled out a five-pound note. He passed it to her. As he did, he looked at her face. She was heavily made up, with bright red lipstick and heavy eye shadow. She must have been attractive when she was younger, but time, and probably a couple of kids, had taken their toll. Michael drained the glass in one swallow.

"Are you having another, 'cause if you are, I wouldn't mind another half of bitter myself." Michael spun around to see who had spoken. He looked down into the face of a wizened old man wearing scruffy clothes and clutching an empty beer glass. Michael immediately recognised him as one of the residents of Armstrong Terrace. The man spoke again. "Don't often see you around here at this time of day. Don't often come here this early myself as a matter of fact, but something's going on so I've come out of the way. I don't want to get mixed up in that sort of thing."

"What sort of thing?" Michael asked as he turned and nodded to the barmaid.

"You know, drugs and things. I noticed a chap hanging around earlier so I asked him what he was up to. He told me he was a copper and they were going to do a raid down the terrace so I should keep out of the way. Bet they're going to number three, that kid in there has always got people calling. They turn up at all hours of the day and night. They sometimes knock me up asking where they can buy stuff. Hope the bastard gets nicked."

The barmaid returned with a large whisky and half of bitter. The old man grabbed the beer and, without saying thank you, sauntered over to where a group of men his age, were playing dominos. Michael gripped the glass of whisky with both hands. It was the only way he could stop them from shaking. His mind was whirling. His suspicions had been correct, the police were at the house, they were onto them. He knew the drugs raid was just a cover to keep the locals away. He had to get home and tell Melinda the bad news. He slipped out of the pub and made his way back to the bus stop.

Chapter 60

Bill checked his watch again, it showed 1915. *Nearly time*, he thought. He brought the radio handset that had been resting in his lap up to his mouth. He pressed the transmit button and spoke. "All units stand by. Keep your eyes open. Things should start happening soon."

Back at the MIR Peter overheard the message. "I hope you're right, Bill," he said under his breath. This was the hardest part, the waiting.

1945. Peter had heard nothing from the scene. He was loathe to disturb them but his gut feeling was that something was wrong. He would leave it another fifteen minutes. He saw every one of the fifteen minutes tick by on the office clock. Finally, his patience snapped and he clicked the transmit button on his radio. "Hotel Zero One to Hotel Zero Two a message over."

"Hotel Zero One, pass your message."

"Bill what's happening? I assume not a lot."

"Absolutely nothing," replied Bill. "No one's been near the place. None of the observers have seen anything, looks like it's a no-goer." Bill listened for his boss's reply. He thought how amazing it was that at times like this you could hear 'silence'. His radio crackled slightly then Peter's disappointed voice came through.

"Zero One to Zero Two, give it until 2000 hours then wrap it up and come back to the office."

"Zero Two. Message received and understood. Out."

Simultaneously Peter and Bill threw their radios down in disgust.

By 2030 hours the team were back at the MIR. Peter saw no point to prolonging the agony, he could see the disappointment in everyone's faces. He ordered the team to go home and reassemble the following morning. It looks like they would have to go back to the drawing board. The team drifted away until only Peter and Karen were left. "Fancy a drink?" Karen asked.

"Not tonight thanks, I'm not feeling very sociable at the moment, another time perhaps?"

"Yes. OK. I understand. See you in the morning then," said Karen sadly.

"Yes, good night."

Despite the disappointing end to the day Peter left the office in a cheery mood. *It's an ill wind*, he thought. *At least I get to see Jenny and the kids before they go to bed.*

Chapter 61

When the team assembled the next day the atmosphere in the MIR was subdued. The usual morning banter was missing. Even the 'ever cheerful' Andy was quiet. Peter knew he had to re-motivate his team.

"OK, everybody, listen up," he said. "I know you are all as pissed off as I am with what happened yesterday but we need to reassess our options. I know you're not going to like what I have to say but here goes. In order to get back on track and start to make progress again in this case, we are going to re-check all our information. We are going to look at absolutely everything concerning these murders again. Check fingerprints, autopsy reports, personnel searches, SOCO procedures, even the colour of the dog's fur if necessary. I want no stone left unturned. It is imperative that we re-establish contact with Melinda, and try to arrange another meeting. I want the twenty-four-hour surveillance back in place on both Michael Drake and Armstrong Terrace. We're missing something, I just know we are."

Peter was pleased, but not surprised, with the professional manner that the team took this news with. He was aware of how much work was involved and how tedious going over previously completed work was. It had to be done though. He was convinced old-fashioned police work was the answer to these crimes. It might be long and laborious but it usually turned up something. He would keep his fingers crossed. The team seemed to go onto auto-pilot. The senior members, who had dealt with this type of problem before, soon organised the less experienced ones. Peter noticed that officers who had dealt with specific enquiries the first time around were given different tasks. He knew that sometimes a new pair of eyes saw things that might have been inadvertently missed during the original investigations. Hopefully time would tell.

For the next three days nothing new was uncovered. Despite numerous attempts to contact her, Melinda failed to respond. The surveillance teams reported nothing unusual from the house and Michael Drake seemed to be carrying on with his life as normal. Pete could feel the frustration within the teams beginning to build. At five o'clock he called a halt to the day's proceedings and took everyone to the local pub for a swift drink before heading off home. He felt they deserved a bit of a boost for all their hard work.

On the fourth morning, as Peter was going over some administration work with Alan Stanton, one of the junior members of the team approached him. "Could I have a word with you please, sir?" The voice belonged to DC Ian Walker. Peter knew that Ian had been assigned the unenviable task of going over the SOCO reports. "Yes Ian, what is it?"

"Well, sir, I think I may have found something." Peter immediately stopped what he was doing and gave the young DC his undivided attention. "I've been looking at all the fingerprint reports from the case. We have them from all over, literally hundreds. There are prints from the scrap yards, recovered cars, the house and of course the toxicology lab. Because the few that came back from the national register as recorded were checked and discounted, nothing else was really done with the prints after that. I got to thinking about this and came at it from a different angle."

"Go on," said Peter.

"Well, I ran a comparison check on all the prints we had. I wanted to see if any of them were found in more than one place. Guess what? One was."

Peter began to feel the hairs on the back of his neck stand up. Could this be something they had missed? Was this the break they were looking for? He took a deep breath and asked, "What did you find, Ian?"

"The two prints that matched were, the partial one from the riding crop found under the floorboards at Armstrong Terrace, and one from the toxicology lab."

"Whose print was it from the lab?"

"That print came from Michael Drake sir."

A sick feeling came over Peter as the reality sank in. So Michael Drake had been at Armstrong Terrace at some time and handled the riding crop. *He has a great deal of explaining to do*, thought Peter.

"Andy, contact the team who are covering Drake, find out where he is. Karen, prepare an interview room. Once we find Mr Drake, we'll need to bring him in for a chat." Whilst Peter was thinking of what else they would need to do the fax machine began to bleep. An official looking piece of A4 size paper rolled off the machine. One of the team collected the paper and stood reading it. He paled and handed the paper to Bill Hodge. "What's this?" Bill asked.

"I was doing some more checks on Drake's previous

girlfriend, Adele Tomlinson. Thanks to a very efficient clerk at the national records office, we established that she changed her name, by deed poll, when she was sixteen. Her original name was Melinda Brown." Peter gasped.

"Do we have an address for her?"

"We do, but you won't like it."

"Where is it?"

"Larch Lane Cemetery Bolton. Her death certificate recorded the cause of death as suicide by hanging seven years ago. She was found in the cellar of a derelict house by a group of addicts who sometimes went there to shoot up. I've checked the original investigation report and nothing suspicious was found at the scene.

"Oh. Fuck!" Peter exclaimed.

Chapter 62

The room was deadly quiet as everyone tried to take in the latest pieces of information. The silence was finally broken by the crackling of a radio transmission. Karen picked up the radio and responded to the call. She listened intently then, after acknowledging the message, she turned to Pete. "That was a message from the surveillance team watching Michael Drake. They say he is still at his home address. Apparently, he hasn't been out for a couple of days."

"Thanks. Right, let's go and pay Mr Drake another visit, shall we? Bill, Karen, Andy, you're with me. The rest of you stay here in case we need anything. Make sure the radio is monitored." Peter headed out of the office closely followed by the other three. *Could this be it?* he thought.

The traffic was heavy, making the journey to Drake's flat even longer than normal. When they arrived at the address, Peter was met by the surveillance team. They informed him that nothing had changed. Drake was still inside. Peter deployed two officers at the bottom of the stairs leading up to the flat. He wanted all escape routes covered in case Drake made a run for it. The rest of the squad were spread out around the main building. Peter and Bill approached the door to the flat, stopped and listened. The sound of soft music could be heard from inside. Taking a deep breath Peter knocked on the door.

After a few moments Peter heard the sound of a key being turned and saw the door handle slowly turn. The door opened a fraction and a grotesque face peered out. "Yes, can I help you?" Peter was taken aback for a moment when his mind registered what his eyes were seeing. The face was familiar. It was the deathly white make up and the vivid red lips that threw him. He moved forward and pushed against the door. The figure behind the door retreated, allowing Peter to enter the flat. Again, he studied the person standing in front of him. It was obviously male, but he was dressed in a tight-fitting red 'T' shirt and a pencil slim black skirt. He wore black stockings and stiletto heeled shoes. A long slim cheroot hung from the fingers of his left hand.

"Just force your way in, why don't you? I hope you have search-warrant? Michael told me you might turn up. You are the police I assume?" the male asked as he walked across the room and sat down in an armchair. "If you're looking for Michael, well you're too late, he's gone. He left ages ago and I know for sure he'll never come back! He was a waste of space anyway."

Peter was totally confused by now. He knew the person in front of him was obviously Michael Drake but he was at a loss as to why he looked and behaved like this. He decided to play along and see where it took him. "Do you mind if I ask you a couple of questions, miss?"

"Feel free, I've nothing to hide."

"Would you mind telling me your name?"

"Of course, my name is Melinda Brown!"

Chapter 63
Six Weeks Later

Peter was sat at a corner table in the Ferret and Sprout public house. Untouched in front of him was a pint of Tetley Smooth and a glass of orange juice. The door to the pub opened and in walked Amir Patel, the police FME. Amir spotted Peter, smiled, and walked over to the table. Removing his coat and laying it across a spare chair, he sat down, raised the glass of orange juice and said, "Cheers."

"Cheers," replied Peter. "I owe you that." Both men took a long swig of their drinks and let out a long breath as they replaced the glasses on the table. "What's the latest, my friend?"

"Well, as you can imagine, it's very complicated, but if I start from the beginning it may be easier for you to follow. As you are aware when Michael Drake was a child, he lived at the Weybrooke Children's Home. Whilst there he was subject, as were most of the children, to repeated sexual abuse by the two senior members of staff, a particularly vicious female and a weak but perverted male. Unfortunately, despite a protracted investigation and search, the two were never located. More's the pity, I think!

"Drake had a special friend at the home, Melinda Brown.

This friendship continued after the home was closed and they went out into the big wide world. They lived together but their relationship was not sexual. Their past prevented them from having a normal life as a couple. I believe, however, that they did love each other deeply as a result of what they had been through as children. They relied on each other for strength and support. Unfortunately for them, things started to go wrong a few years ago. Melinda's mental state started to deteriorate badly, so badly, in fact that she left Michael and ended up committing suicide as you discovered. Michael was devastated of course, and he would never accept that she was dead. His mind refused to believe she was gone. He started to imagine she was still here. To him, of course, she was, and she again became an integral part of his life. He carried on as normal, working, going to the gym etc. Gradually Melinda's personality became part of Michael's. He developed the classic symptoms of schizophrenia, social withdrawal, hallucinations, bizarre behaviour and sleep disturbance.

"Schizophrenics always develop a dominant side, and in this case, Melinda became the stronger. The Melinda personality used Michael to help her exact revenge for the previous torment they had suffered. He used his technical knowledge of the internet to develop a website to attract a specific type of male. You know what they did, Peter. They attracted, then killed, the same type of men they perceived to be like their tormentors at the home."

"We were lucky in some respects," said Peter. "If that dog handler had not had an inquisitive pooch, it could have been years and many more deaths before we discovered what was happening."

"Yes," replied Amir. "It was a very clever way to dispose

of bodies without them being found."

"What will happen to Drake now?"

"I have spoken to the physiatrist who is dealing with Drake. She says that with intensive treatment he could improve over the years but he will never fully recover. His defence team will enter a plea of insanity and he will most likely be confined in a secure mental hospital for the rest of his life. People like Michael Drake are not really criminals though. Yes, he committed seven despicable murders but he was the victim of our institutionalised cruelty and as such, understandably, looked for revenge.

As we saw, seven innocent, all be it perverted, men suffered the 'Backlash' from the cruelty that this very troubled young man suffered in his childhood.

Peter nodded his agreement as Amir asked if he would like another drink. Just as he was about to answer, his phone rang. He hit the answer button. "Hello, DI Bridle."

"Hello, boss. It's Bill Hodge. We've got a body in a house on Walton Grove."

Peter waved to Amir. "Forget the drink," he said. "It looks like we're going to be busy again."

The End.